BEST OF THE BEST

I0710046

BEST OF THE BEST

A Colorado Black Diamonds Novel

EMILY SILVER

To all the badass women out there made to feel less than you are.
Take up space. You're worth it.

If bullying is a triggering subject for you, please note that while there are brief mentions of past bullying touched on in this book, there is nothing that is described in detail on page.

<3 Emily

Chapter One

BEXLEY

"Bexley. What do you have to say about the team's recent success?"

"Coach Barney has been leading the team well. Hollins and Williams and the whole line is gelling well. I like what I'm seeing out there."

"The outgoing GM set you up nicely to continue the winning seasons that Black Diamonds fans are used to. What do you have to say about that?"

Grinding my jaw and crossing one leg over the other, I steady my thoughts before shouting the first thing that comes to mind. I don't know why I started these weekly press conferences.

Maybe to prove myself? Even after we won the Stanley Cup last year, everyone simply praised the outgoing GM for setting me up for success. It wasn't something I got any credit for.

So here I am. Bright and early on a Monday morning, answering the same old questions over and over again.

Like why the team is successful…almost in spite of me.

"I've been around this game since I was born. I know

hockey, probably better than most people. So yes, Paulson set this team up to win the cup last year. Changes in leadership can always affect a team. Our guys are a strong group and they do a great job pushing out distractions. I have every faith that they will keep the outside noise out of the locker room so they can focus on our ultimate goal of bringing another championship home to Denver."

"And what about Fields's recent injury?"

Jesus, it's like they don't even hear me when I talk. I really should cancel these press conferences. Tell them all to fuck off.

If only…

"He is recovering well, and hopefully he'll be back to the player we all know and love soon."

Even if he isn't back to full strength yet.

Another reporter pops up from the back of the press room. It's nothing but concrete walls painted in the team's colors with our sponsors plastered behind me. "Do you feel the league should have punished Graham Fisher?"

"Was it an intentional hit?" I cross my arms, thinking about the question. "I don't believe it was. It's one of those unfortunate series of events that happens on the ice. Hopefully Noah will be back into top form soon."

Because anything less than that and I don't want to think about his future with the team.

"Do you think the team will be gunning for Fisher the next time they play the Knights?"

I scoff. "I certainly hope not. I don't condone that kind of behavior on the ice."

"And off it?"

"I think that's all we have time for today," Cassie cuts in, strutting into the press room. "We appreciate you all being here today."

I watch as the room empties out around me, and I breathe a sigh of relief.

"Why do you do this to yourself, Bex?" Cassie asks once the room is empty.

I grab the glass of water and take a hearty gulp. "You know why."

She rolls her eyes at me as I kick my feet up on the table. The Black Diamonds logo hangs heavy behind me. The weight of it always seems to be pressing down on my chest.

I was handed the reins from my father last year, and I don't want to disappoint him. Or his legacy.

"The men don't do this," Cassie scoffs.

"Because they don't have to. You show up with a dick and they assume you know how to do this job. Even if you don't have the first clue how to do it."

"Would it help if I told you you're doing a good job?"

I smile back at my communications director. "Not really since I sign your paychecks."

"Technically accounting does. And technically it's not a real check anymore." She laughs.

I roll my eyes at her and stand. "Whatever. I have a meeting with Coach Barney I need to get to."

"Well, I think you're doing good."

Cassie follows me as I head down the hall in the practice rink toward the coaches' offices. A few of the guys are coming off the ice from practice.

I stand back and watch. They're giving each other shit about something, it looks like, laughing and joshing around.

This is why I love doing what I do. I grew up around the game. With my dad playing for the Black Diamonds, this team means everything to me.

My eyes connect with our newest goalie, Nick Brooks-

Young. A flush creeps up his cheeks as he tries to scurry even faster toward the locker room.

A feat considering he is in his goalie gear.

A smirk creeps up my lips. I think back to our earlier interaction from this week. It's like he takes one look at me and he can't string two words together.

I'm not that intimidating, am I?

I don't rule with fear. I don't see the point in making people scared of you. So I can't quite figure out why Nick scurries away from me.

The rest of the day goes by without incident.

Meeting after meeting. A never-ending list of phone calls to return.

"Bex?" Anna, my assistant comes into my office, my bag in her hand.

"You wanted me to let you know when it's seven."

"Shit," I mutter.

I glance at my watch and it's seven on the dot. I have a date tonight. Not that I am overly excited about it, but at least I am putting myself out there.

"Can you cancel?" I ask.

"Nope." Anna looks at me with a satisfied smile on her face.

"Aren't you supposed to do what I ask of you?" I laugh, dropping the papers in my hand.

Even if I left now, in Denver traffic, it would take me at least thirty minutes to get across town.

Is it even worth it?

"If you want to cancel your date, you can do it. I was told to remind you of it so you could make it in time."

"I should go." There's not much conviction in my voice.

"But…"

Anna knows me too well, having started with me last year when I got promoted.

"But I need to review the new league initiatives on player safety that we'll be voting on at the next league-wide meetings."

Anna rolls her eyes at me.

"Do you want me to order dinner instead?"

I give her a consolatory smile. "Can you? You can take off."

"I stay until you leave," Anna says.

"You're the best assistant, you know that?"

She nods, dropping my bag onto the chair in the small sitting area in my office. Furnished with a small sofa, I have to admit I've spent a night or two here in the office. Maybe I made it too cozy. But I wanted to be surrounded by a zen space that made it easier to get lost in my work.

Warm grays and pinks are exactly what I wanted.

"You should give me a raise then." Anna laughs, heading back out to her desk.

It's something I've heard before, even though I pay her very well.

Grabbing my phone, I fire off a text to my date for the night. Maybe if I was more excited, I wouldn't have to be reminded to leave.

A sweet face pops into mind. A stubble-lined one with dark hair and deep-blue, expressive eyes.

Why in the world am I thinking about our goalie? I don't need to be having these thoughts right now. I need to let this guy down gently and go back to work.

Work won't keep me warm at night. I know I need more of a work-life balance, but until then…it's just another day in the life of a hockey GM.

Chapter Two

NICK

The feel of the ice. The posts behind me. The glove in my hand.

This. This is why I love hockey. Why I love playing goalie. Even as another slapshot comes flying at me, I don't care. I swiftly pluck it from the air in my glove and drop it onto the ice, passing it to one of my guys.

"Great stop, little Nicky! You're unbeatable."

Cash elbows me in the side with his stick as the whistle blows practice to a pause.

"Don't jinx me. The last thing I need is to fuck up my shoulder again."

"Or just have issues with your entire body." Noah winces as he skates over to us and steals my water bottle for a swig.

"Your leg still giving you trouble?" I ask.

"Can't seem to make this nagging injury I got after that hit from Fisher go away."

"I think that's called getting old," I chirp.

Noah flips me the bird as best he can while still wearing his gloves. "Fuck off. I'm only twenty-nine."

"That's ancient in hockey years," Cash tells him.

"You're older than I am," Noah huffs.

"Piper keeps me young."

"Oh gross!" Noah mocks gagging. "That's my sister."

"You made it gross. I didn't."

"Could both of you maybe stop?" I grab my water bottle back from Cash and take my own sip. "You're ruining my zen."

They look at each other before looking at me. "Is this how you stay so calm in the crease?" Cash asks.

I nod, tapping my stick against the left post behind me. "Yes. Because otherwise bickering idiots on the ice would distract me."

"Are you calling us idiots?" Noah asks.

"Never." I shake my head, smiling at him. "Not you two."

"You guys done chatting, or are you going to waste our time all day? I have plans tonight," Troy says as he skates over, breaking up the conversation.

Looking behind him, the rest of the guys are still standing around. The coaches have their heads buried over an iPad. My guess is they're reviewing film from our game last night.

It was about as easy a win as we can come by. Atlanta wasn't prepared for us. With their starting center out for the season with an ACL tear, they were skating from behind all night.

It made for a 5-1 win.

Even so, that's no reason to ease up on the accelerator. We've got a long way to go if we want to make the playoffs this season. We won't settle for anything less than making it to the playoffs after winning the cup last season.

"Alright men, let's do a few more drills and then we'll hit the weight room. Take it easy. I want everyone rested up for tomorrow. Noah,"—Coach Barney glances over at our small group—"see the trainers. I want your knee looked at."

"Roger that."

"I thought your knee was feeling better?" Troy asks.

"It's fine. I wish everyone would stop making such a big deal of it."

I watch the three of them head back to center ice as the goalie coach skates over to me. "Feeling up for some glove drills?"

"Hit me where it hurts," I tell him, slinging my helmet back down into place.

It's one of my least favorite drills, but I can't tell him that. By the time I'm done with these, I'm exhausted. They work though, so I suck it up, catching each puck with my glove only as they're fired off toward me.

This is one of the things that made me realize how good I was in high school. I had the hand-eye coordination needed for being an NHL goalie.

It wasn't something I ever set out to do. But when I started playing pickup games with Noah on his weekends home in college, I couldn't deny the pull of it. The lure of the game.

My dads enrolled me in the club team in high school, and I haven't looked back since. Didn't hurt that it kept people off my back too.

"Alright, Nick. Hit the showers."

"Thank fuck," I mutter, skating off the ice as the backup goaltender goes in. I'm not about to argue with him.

"Nick. You looked good out there today."

"Ms. Hart."

I draw up short of the tunnel, staring down the team owner's daughter. Our general manager.

Bexley Hart. She is a force to be reckoned with. Not only is she the only female GM in the league, but she's also the youngest.

"Please, call me Bexley."

I give her a shy smile because it's all I can do to not look like a blubbering idiot. This woman is fucking gorgeous.

Long, dark hair flows down her back over the blazer she's wearing. Lashes kiss her cheeks. Plump lips begging to be kissed.

Not that I've thought about it. Not at all.

"You had some great saves out there." Bexley leans against the wall, giving me a better view to study her.

"I did?" I'm not sure why it comes out as a question. I know I did. I had a killer practice, but when I get around people I'm not comfortable with, I turn into this.

Someone who loses all thought and ends up spewing random words all over the place.

"Of course. It's why we pay you the big bucks."

"Big bucks. Me. Right."

Fidgeting, I take my gloves and helmet off. I need something to do with my hands to try and stop myself from making this worse.

"Even though this is my second season as GM, I'm still learning the ropes around here, but you're one of the breakout stars from your draft class. Picked in the middle of the pack and not expected to get much playing time—"

"Until Anderson went down."

It isn't the kind of hit I like to see toward anyone. His legs got taken out from under him while another guy crashed into him from behind. It broke his femur in two spots. He was never quite the same after that.

Even though he isn't playing anymore, he still offers me his guidance.

"I hear he's been helping you."

"Yup."

Bex smiles at me because I can't elaborate any more than that. "I hear he studies film with you. Quite nice when he's no longer with the team." She quirks a perfect brow at me.

"Really nice. He's good at it. Helps me. A lot."

Words, Nick, words.

"Good, I'm glad." Bexley looks off to the ice where the other guys are still running through drills. "I don't want to keep you. Just came to see how the guys are doing today."

"Right."

I wish I could be more impressive around this woman. She's a badass as far as I'm concerned. It only makes my blabbering worse around her.

I'm not your typical egotistical hockey player. I'd rather stay out of the spotlight. It's quite the conundrum of a job —loving what I do, but not wanting to be in the limelight.

I want to come off as the confident goalie I am between the pipes. Usually it's not this bad. But somehow, being in the presence of someone so…so powerful and assured only makes it worse for me.

The sounds of sticks hitting the ice tells me practice is wrapping up. I need to hit the weight room to wind down before heading home.

"Gentlemen. Looking good out there. Looks like we could have another great season this year," Bex calls out as the guys start skating off the ice.

"Hope so," Troy tells her matter-of-factly. "Team is strong this year."

"That's what I like to hear."

Players jostle me as they go, pushing me right into Bexley. In my skates and gear, I tower over her. She is small compared to me, but that is not the way I'd describe her.

"Sorry," I whisper to her.

A smile tilts up one side of her mouth. "It's okay."

I shouldn't be thinking about what a cute smile that is. Or how good she smells. *For God sake's, Nick, she's your GM*, I chide myself.

It's overwhelming being this close to her. It shouldn't be, though. I need to push these thoughts out of my head. The last thing I need is to think about Bexley this way. It will only make it worse for me the next time I see her.

Just because she smiled at you and complimented your play doesn't mean she likes you. She does it for everyone.

"Bex. Glad you're here. Ready to talk numbers?" Coach Barney asks her.

Jumping away from her, I spin on my skates and head toward the locker room, trying to shake off the Bexley-induced stupor.

"Nice talking to you, Nick," she calls out after me.

"You too, Ms. Hart."

"What'd I tell you?" Bexley asks.

"To call you Bexley."

"That's right, Nick."

"Okay, Bexley. I'll see you around."

I watch her go as she starts chatting with Coach.

What an idiot, I chastise myself.

It's not that I have a crush on Bexley. I mean, in what world could the two of us ever be together? Forget the fact that she's the general manager; she's more than a decade older than me.

I need to get rid of these feelings and buckle down on hockey. It's still early in the season. We have a cup to defend. Bexley Hart?

Forget about it.

"What are you staring at, Nicky?" Cash wraps an arm

around my shoulders and pulls me toward the locker room with him.

"Nothing."

The crap I would get from him if he knew I had a crush? I would never hear the end of it. This is why I keep my mouth shut in the locker room. I hear the chirping that goes on.

Keeping my head down is the easiest way to do that. Even if the fans come after me for any loss. Staying out of the limelight makes it easier.

Sure, I'm a team player, but I still keep to myself.

Cash's eyes follow where mine are tracking. He's smarter than I give him credit for. "Like the older woman, huh?"

I shake my head, pushing him off of me. "Nah. Just trying to figure out how much of a break I can get before hitting the weights."

"Coach Barney will make tomorrow hell for all of us if you're late," Cash tells me.

Thank God he bought that. Because I don't want to give away what I'm thinking or feeling toward the person I was really looking at.

Bexley.

Not that I have any feelings toward her. None whatsoever.

Hockey needs to be my only focus.

Not a GM that turns me into a rambling idiot.

Hockey. Only hockey.

Chapter Three

NICK

I swig my water as I skate off the ice to booming cheers from the crowd. Fuck, this feels good. Shutouts, while not uncommon in the league, haven't happened against Dallas this season.

To be the first one to stop them from putting points on the board? Yeah, it feels fucking great.

I wave to the crowd decked out in navy and light blue as I disappear down the tunnel. I'm sure I'll be roped into talking to the press, but for now, I'm going to ride this high.

"Hell yeah, Nicky!"

"Way to go!"

The guys welcome me into the locker room like a king, causing a blush to creep out on my cheeks. I like keeping my head down and playing a good game. It's how I've always wanted to play my game.

"Already kicking ass and taking names," Troy calls out as I head to the wooden stall of my locker, ready to shuck off these pads.

"Okay, okay." I wave him off, dropping into the seat, lit up from above.

"Hey, take the praise when you can. That was a fan-fucking-tastic game, Nicky." Cash snaps his towel my direction before hitting the showers.

"Glad you were able to make the save when they stole the puck." Noah winces.

He's still been struggling since getting injured. It's hard watching him play when I know the player he can be. His speed and strength hasn't been there this season.

"We all have a bad game. That's why it's a team sport."

"All thanks to you."

I grab my towel, bypassing the Black Diamonds logo that takes up the center of the locker room floor—it's bad luck to walk on it—and hit the showers, letting the steam wash over my tired muscles. With tonight's win, we're in a solid position this season. We started strong, something every Stanley Cup champion wants to do, and we've carried the momentum this far.

Is it too much to already hope for back-to-back wins?

Rapping my knuckles on the tile—just in case—I turn off the water and head back into the locker room.

As soon as I've changed into my game suit, and then talked to the press, Coach Barney is calling for everyone's attention. Bexley is standing next to him. She's always down here after postgame interviews.

Encouraging the team. Lifting us up when needed. She's the best GM out there as far as I'm concerned, no matter what the press says about her.

Doesn't hurt that she's easy on the eyes. I only wish I didn't stare at her every time she makes an appearance.

Her gaze sweeps across the locker room, stopping for a moment longer on me. Did I imagine it, or did her smile get a little bigger?

Probably only because of the shutout and no other reason.

I don't know how I can be the confident player between the pipes and turn into a high school kid with a crush around this woman.

Coach's words bring me out of my self-flagellation.

"Alright. Our player of the game goes to Nick. Great job on shutting out an excellent team. Dallas is going to be a team that will make a deep playoff run, so fantastic job," Coach Barney calls me out, clapping loudly as the rest of the team does the same. "We've got a hard stretch of games coming up, and I don't want anyone getting complacent. Keep working hard and playing the hockey I know you're capable of, and we'll go far."

Nods and agreements are heard all around the locker room.

"Enjoy the win tonight, but not too much, and I'll see you all at one for a light workout. You've earned the morning off."

"Hell yeah!" Noah shouts, swinging an arm around me. "Nothing like skipping practice after a win. Thanks, man."

"I'll try for shutouts more often then." I laugh.

"Nicky, you coming out to celebrate? A shutout? You can't say no," Cash tells me.

I roll my eyes at him as I grab my keys and wallet and stuff them into my pockets. "Fine."

"Don't sound so excited," Noah says. "Oreo will be fine."

I point at him. "This is why I'm a better parent than you."

"Doesn't your neighbor keep an eye on him during game nights?" Troy asks. "I mean, he's a bunny. Will he know if you're not there?"

"Troy, I really hope you're not going to have kids anytime soon," I poke at him. "You'd make a terrible dad."

"A bunny is different than kids. If Ang hadn't received that big promotion, I'd be working on kids now."

I shudder, not wanting to think about that. As much as I want to be an uncle, this is the part I don't need to know.

"Remember, none of that," Cash tells him, wrapping an arm around my shoulders and slapping my chest. "You'll scar poor Nicky here."

"You guys suck sometimes, you know that?"

"Tell us that when we're buying you drinks at the bar."

THE BAR IS LOUD. It's one of the few that is close to the rink that allows us privacy after the games. We can drink without worrying who is going to come up to us and ask for autographs or a picture.

It's the epitome of a sports bar with TVs lining the private room in the back. Black leather booths take up the walls with round tables in the center. Neon signs from different beers light up the room. Jerseys from Denver's greatest athletes fill in the remaining space.

My dad's and Noah's dad's included. It used to be trippy, but not anymore.

Noah is shooting the shit with some of the guys while Cash and Troy are both wrapped up with Piper and Angie.

They are so loved up that sometimes it's hard to watch. Especially when I wish I had that.

"Hey, Nicky's glass is empty. Someone needs to get him another drink!" Cash calls out from his seat next to me. "Our hero of the hour needs a shot!"

"Cash," I mutter. "It wasn't that big of a deal."

"A shutout against Dallas? We're going to celebrate that tonight. You did good, kid."

I groan. I hate when they call me kid. It makes me feel so much younger than my twenty-three.

Not that I've ever felt young. I grew up fast, always being on the wrong side of bullies in middle school. I had to be smarter than they were if I wanted to survive.

One of the servers comes back with a pitcher of beer and Cash tops off my glass.

"Here's to Nicky!" he shouts, everyone raising and clinking their glasses.

"It was a good night," Angie tells me from across the booth. "I love seeing you guys win."

Troy drops a kiss on her cheek, causing her to blush.

God, I wish I had that. I ignore the first face that pops into my mind, because I can't have it with *her*. Bexley is so far out of my league, it's not even funny.

"You're quiet tonight, Nick." Piper leans over Cash, talking louder than necessary when it's quieter in the back area of the bar.

"Just thinking."

"About?"

Do I want to tell her? If I tell her, everyone here will know. It's not that I don't want them to know, it's…how will these guys react?

I love them, but they also love giving me shit. I guess that's the downside of being the youngest guy on the team.

"I need you to set me up."

"What?" Piper asks.

"I need you guys to set me up." This time, I put a little more force behind my words. If I'm going to have them do it, I might as well own it.

"What are you talking about?" Troy sputters around his beer. "Where is this coming from?"

"What? I can't want to meet a nice lady?"

"Lady?" Cash laughs. "You're not dating in the fifties."

"Fuck off. You know what I mean."

"Cash, be nice," Piper chastises him, smacking him in the chest.

"The last time Ang tried to set you up, you told her you weren't interested in dating until you were older," Troy tells me.

I roll my eyes, hating that my captain is also my brother-in-law. Of course he remembers everything I've ever told him.

"Because I was still in college. I didn't want to screw up my focus and risk not getting drafted."

"For a prodigy like you?" Noah asks. "Never would've happened."

"I'm serious though. Watching all of you guys together makes me want what you have."

"I don't have that," Noah corrects.

"You could, Strawberry, if you let us set you up too," Cash says.

"Fuck no. I'm just fine on my own." Noah acts like it's the worst thing in the world to want to be with someone.

"You're not getting any younger," Troy tells him.

Noah flips him off.

Angie, ignoring all of them, turns to me. "You know it wasn't as easy as snapping our fingers and us finding what we have, right?"

"I know." It's not like I don't know what Angie and Piper both went through to find what they have now. Cheating boyfriends and family feuds? I know this. But it doesn't mean I don't want to try and find something. "I just… You're all settled. Happy. I want that too."

They all share sappy looks, and it has me swigging down more of my beer.

"Are you not happy with me and Oreo?" Noah asks,

looking affronted. "I'm beginning to think we're not good enough for you."

I roll my eyes at the dramatics of my best friend. "What, I can't have my best friend, bunny, and a girlfriend?"

"You know, if you post a picture of you with Oreo on a dating app, everyone will eat that up," Troy states.

"Or they would eat him up because he's a hockey player and way too shy for all those women who would be interested," Cash tells me.

"Jesus. You guys really aren't making a good case for me here."

"Sorry." Piper scoots over Cash's lap to take the spot next to me. "Look, I think I have someone that you would like."

"Oh yeah?" I ask.

Piper tucks a lock of blonde hair behind her ear and tells me about her. "Her name is Caroline. We went to school together. She was always nice to me, and I don't think she's that into hockey."

"Seriously? She's not into hockey?" Noah asks.

Piper rolls her eyes at her brother. "There is more to life than hockey."

Cash claps a hand over her mouth as they all gasp. I can't help but laugh at how dramatic they can be.

"Careful, Piper." Cash nips at her neck.

"Gross, Cash. That's my sister," Noah complains.

"You guys." Piper pulls Cash's hand from her mouth and turns back to me. "Ignore them, Nick. I know you don't want someone that is all about hockey. You want someone more balanced."

"I do."

The less someone knows about hockey, the better. It's

always hard to know if someone wants me for me, or if they want me for my position on the team.

Hockey might be a big part of my life, but it isn't my whole life. I know this will end for me one day. I take a beating every game. Pucks flying at me, knees creaking more and more every time I move.

If I find someone who doesn't follow the game, I have a better chance of them not being a puck bunny.

No matter where we go, women always seem to find us after the game. I hate being an object to them. They could trade out any player and it wouldn't matter to them. They're a small minority, but it still rubs me the wrong way.

I want someone who wants me for me. Who is going to respect me. Who will look past the glove and stick and see me for me.

Just like I'll see them for who they really are.

"I'll send you her number," Piper tells me. "You'll like her. I promise."

"To Nicky and dating!" Angie raises her glass and everyone toasts to that, but I only groan.

Do I want this? Yes. Do I want all of these guys in my business every step of the way with it? Maybe. Probably not. No.

But if it means I can find what they have, then I guess I'll have to suck it up.

Because goalies and general managers aren't meant to be together.

Chapter Four

NICK

CASH

Don't be nervous

NICK

I'm not nervous

TROY

I can feel your nerves from here

NOAH

She won't bite…unless you want her to <<winky emoji>>

Not helpful <<middle finger emoji>>

NOAH

But are you more relaxed now?

No

CASH

You have dated before, right?

I don't know why I asked you guys to help

TROY

It's because you love us <<kissy face emoji>>

Do I?

TROY

You have to love me

Only because you married my sister

TROY

And here I thought I was your favorite person on the team!

NOAH

Hey, that's me! I'm his bestie

CASH

Shouldn't it be me because I set him up on the date?

NOAH

You don't win by default, Willy

CASH

And you don't win because you've known him the longest

NOAH

That's exactly why I should win! Nick, tell him

I'm ignoring you guys

TROY

What? Why?

CASH

It's because of Noah. See, you made it worse

NOAH

Fucker! I did not

It's because I'm on a date and don't need you guys arguing over who I love most

CASH

Well, Caroline should be there soon. Don't fuck it up. Piper likes her

I'm not going to <<eye roll emoji>>

TROY

Be interested in her. Ask good questions

What is a good question?

CASH

Something that shows you're listening

Wow, thanks captain obvious

NOAH

Seriously, I don't know how you won my sister over with advice like that

CASH

Do you really want to know? <<eyebrow waggle emoji>>

NOAH

<<vomit emoji vomit emoji vomit emoji>>

And that's my cue to leave you idiots to yourselves

CASH

Good luck, you fucker

NOAH

Asshole!

TROY

Hey!

You guys deserve it

I can't help the smile on my face as I shove my phone into my pocket. The buzzing won't stop. The three of them can really get going when they want to.

I sip on the small glass of bourbon, taking in the quiet of the upscale bar around me. It's not my usual place—all dark brown leather seats with dim lighting and candles on each table. There's a room specifically for people smoking cigars—like it could be right out of a scene from a show set in the 1950s. Everyone from the wait staff to the hosts are all wearing the same outfit—impeccably pressed white shirt, black bowtie, and black pants.

It's perfect for what I wanted tonight. I didn't want to be seen tonight as a professional hockey player.

Because regardless of the guys incessant chirping, I really am crap at dates. I do my best to steel my nerves, but it's not really working.

It's not like I haven't dated. I had a girlfriend in college. But she hated the fact that I played hockey. She couldn't wrap her head around the fact that someone so smart—her words, not mine—would willingly put themselves in the goal every time there was a game.

First dates have never been my thing. Maybe I should be used to the awkwardness by now, but I'm not. I hate it. I never know what to say. I turn into a rambling idiot and scare the woman off within ten minutes. Five if I'm really on point.

I groan, sucking down another sip of the amber liquid.

I best slow down; getting drunk won't be the best first impression.

"Nick? What are you doing here?" A familiar voice startles me as I look up from my drink.

"Uhh, what? I mean, Ms. Hart?"

So much for not turning into a rambling idiot.

"Please, call me Bexley."

"B-Bexley."

I can see her fighting the smirk on her face. As if I wasn't already nervous about tonight—no matter what I told the guys—now I'm worried because the team's GM is here. At the most out-of-place bar I could've picked.

What are the odds?

"Hi."

I blow out a breath, finally answering her question. "I'm here for a date. Hi, hello, hey." I wave awkwardly at her.

Fuck. Me.

I want to reach out and smack myself. If this is how the night is going to go, I should leave now. Sure, I was nervous before, but now someone I know, well, know of, is here and I feel like I'm on display. Almost like she's going to watch this entire date go down and report back to everyone how it goes.

"Oh, okay. Well, have fun."

"You too."

She gives me another smile before walking past me toward the bar. I track her with my eyes. There's something about her. The way she walks.

Bexley Hart is confident. Every single person is turning their head to watch her. She commands the room. Bexley was handed the reins to the team two seasons ago, right after I got drafted. Ever since then, I've been intrigued by her. The power she wields is matched by very few, and no other woman runs a team in this league.

The easy presence about her draws me in. It's something I wish I had. The only reason people take notice of me is my stature. That and I'm the starting goalie for the Black Diamonds.

She takes a spot at the bar, under one of the old Edison bulbs hanging down, and the bartender is there right away, pouring her drink.

If only I were that confident.

I wish her confidence would rub off on me right about now. I could use a healthy dose of it before my date shows up. Not whatever it is that I'm currently feeling.

Nerves? Excitement? Fear?

"Hi." A pretty redhead stands over me at the table. "Are you Nick?"

"Umm, Nick. Yes," is my response. *Off to a great start there, Nicky*, I chastise myself.

She tucks a strand of hair behind her ear. "Hi. I'm Caroline."

"Nice to meet you."

My good manners kick in and I stand, pulling out the chair for her.

"Piper has told me a lot about you."

"She has?"

From what little Piper has told me, they were friends at school together. They see each other every now and then, but that's all I really know about her.

Dropping into the seat, Caroline flags down the passing waiter and orders a glass of wine.

"Instead of me telling you what I know about you, why don't you tell me about yourself?"

I gulp down another sip of bourbon, feeling my palms

begin to sweat. It feels like a question someone would ask at a job interview.

"Well, I uh, play hockey."

"I know you do. Tell me about it."

Caroline leans over the table, her face glowing in the dim candlelight. It's not that she's not pretty, but seeing her eyes closer up, it looks like she has a goal in mind for tonight.

To bag a hockey player?

If this woman turns out to be a puck bunny, I'm going to be pissed.

"I play for the Black Diamonds."

A glass of wine is set down in front of her and she takes a hearty sip. It makes me feel like this isn't going well at all.

My eyes drift past her shoulder to the woman staring at me from the bar.

Bexley.

Her arm is casually draped over the back of the leather stool, one leg crossed over the other.

"I know that. What's it like?" Caroline brings my attention back to her. Her fingers are tracing a pattern in the dark wood of the table.

"It's great most days. Except when we lose. People can get shitty when we lose."

"I don't really watch much hockey," she tells me.

"Really?"

"The puck going back and forth is too hard to follow for me."

I smile at her. This. Hockey. Hockey is something I can talk about without turning into an idiot.

"For me, it's all about the strategy. Where that person is going to go. Trying to read their every move as they fly down the ice. Are they going to pass the puck? Keep it for themselves? Sometimes, you can sense where they are going to go. Other times, you have to trust your gut and hope you make the right move. The puck can go over your shoulder into the goal in the blink of an eye. I love it."

Caroline's eyes glaze over the more I wax on about hockey.

Shit. Maybe this isn't going so well. The one thing that doesn't make me nervous and I'm losing her.

"Sorry. You don't like hockey." I fidget with the napkin sitting under my glass. "Sometimes I can get carried away. Why don't you tell me about yourself."

"Well, I'm a massage therapist during the day, but an aspiring influencer in my spare time."

I blink, hoping not to look like an idiot. *An aspiring influencer?* What the hell does that mean?

"What does an aspiring influencer do?"

My voice sounds steady to my ears. Thank God, because I wouldn't want her to think I'm being judgmental. But honestly, I don't even know what an aspiring influencer does.

"God, you sound just like my ex."

I wince, leaning back in my chair. "Sorry. I just don't know what they do."

"I influence people to buy things." Caroline tosses her long red hair behind her shoulder. "Then I get paid for it."

"And what kind of things do you sell?"

"Well, I don't sell them. Companies send me stuff for free to try and then I give my opinions for others to buy and then I make commissions off them."

"Okay."

"You don't sound excited by it."

"Sorry, I've just never met anyone who does that, and I don't know much about it."

She rolls her eyes at me. "That's just your nice way of saying I'm trying to be famous without even trying."

"What?" Now I'm confused.

"God, forget my ex. You sound like my parents. Forcing me to make a living doing something I don't want to do."

"I thought you were a massage therapist?"

Caroline waves me off, her pink nails catching in the low light of the bar. "It's not what I want to be. Not really."

"An influencer." I keep my tone light, hoping not to dig myself into a deeper hole.

"Now you're just humoring me." Pink colors her cheeks, like she's getting worked up.

God, I'm messing up this conversation. I don't know where I took a turn into a dangerous territory, but it's not going well.

"I'm not." I hold up my hands, trying to calm her down. "Only trying to learn more about you."

Caroline reaches into a small black bag and pulls out her wallet. "I don't think this is going to work."

"What? You've only been here for"—I glance at my watch, noting the time—"ten minutes."

"And do you really see this working?" She quirks a perfectly manicured brow at me.

"Uhh…"

"See? You don't either. Bye, Nick."

She drops a twenty on the table, gulps down the remainder of her wine, and leaves.

"Bye?" It's more of a question, because what the fuck just happened?

Chapter Five

Watching a train wreck would be less painful than what I'm watching now. When I bumped into Nick and he said he was on a date, I couldn't help peeking over my glass of wine and watching him.

I know I shouldn't. I should let him have his own time. Maybe he's meeting the person he's supposed to be with.

I can't say the same about me. At least his date came. Mine sent a text after I arrived saying he wouldn't be joining me tonight because his fish was sick.

His fish.

Grow a pair and if you don't want to come, just tell me.

Was he intimidated by me? The number of times I've heard this isn't anything new. I've got a thick skin because of it.

Which, judging by what I'm watching, might not be the case for Nick. It's only been a couple of minutes and I think his date is already leaving for the night.

I don't think that could have gone worse.

"Need anything else?" the bartender asks me.

"I'll take another glass and whatever that man is having." I point behind me to Nick.

"Coming right up."

I wait as he pours our drinks and passes them over.

"Thanks."

Grabbing both glasses, I stand and head over to the small table in the corner of the bar.

To say Nick looks shell-shocked is an understatement.

"How'd the big date go?"

I drop down into the seat across from him and pass him his drink. I watch his throat work as he swallows down half of it.

"If I knew, I could tell you." He laughs, but it's full of misery.

"That great, huh?"

Nick rubs a hand over his stubbled jaw. "You saw. It was a disaster from start to finish."

"It was painful to watch, sorry."

"Don't be. I don't even know what happened."

I lean across the table, studying him. His blue eyes are wide, taking everything in around him. "Did you show interest in her interests?"

Nick nods. "She wants to be an influencer, so I asked her about that and she freaked on me."

"An influencer? Really?" It's hard to hide the skepticism from my tone.

"That was the tone I had and she did *not* appreciate it."

"Well, I'm sorry it didn't go well."

"The guys were right," he mutters.

"About what?"

"Me being a disaster at this."

"At dating? I don't think one bad date makes you bad at it. I've had plenty of bad dates. It's just how it goes. At least you showed up. My date texted me to let me know he wasn't coming."

Except, thinking back to how he was when I first got here…is he a disaster? He's fine now, but maybe he's still in a haze from the date ending so fast.

"Maybe when I get to your age I'll be better at it."

"Ouch."

His face reddens and he looks chagrined. "Shit. I didn't mean it that way. I only meant maybe I'll be good like you. More experienced?"

"Assuming you have more dates and don't meet someone before my age."

"Exactly. Shit. That still sounds bad. God, I really am terrible at this."

Nick drops his head into his hands. His shoulders drop as he lets out a long sigh. There's something about Nick that is tender. That makes you want to protect this sweet man at all costs.

Because that's what he is. Sweet. Based on the few interactions I've had with him, and watching him with the team, there isn't an arrogant bone in his body.

I know very little about him, except for the fact that he's our starting goalie and his dad is the best quarterback to ever play in the NFL.

"Maybe you just need some help."

"Help?" he questions, glancing up at me. "With dating? There's no way I'm asking the guys for help. I'll never hear the end of it."

I sip on my wine to hide my smile. It's clear he loves his teammates, even if they are going to give him shit.

It has me blurting out the words that come next without thought.

"Do you want help?"

"From you?" he scoffs.

I nod. "From me, yes. Maybe we could help each other."

Nick's eyes land on me in a curious way. The deep-blue eyes darken as they focus on me and only me. His gaze doesn't stray from me.

"Help each other? Why do you need help?"

"Like I said,"—I shrug a shoulder, sipping on my drink—"my date stood me up."

"And you need my help to get them to show up? Why? You're gorgeous."

I can't hide my smile at his words. I don't think he even knows he said it as he stares back at me. I shift in my chair. It's been a long time since I've been under the gaze of a man.

Does he know the power he commands with that look? If he did, maybe his date wouldn't have been so quick to leave. The way his eyes are assessing me without making me feel cheap? It has goose bumps breaking out over my entire body.

Men like Nick? A sweet guy who actually listens? They don't exist for me. My job has always gotten in the way and they never understand.

When I took over the team, it became my entire life. My dad needed me to step up when the old GM retired.

I eat, sleep, and breathe hockey.

Is it the healthiest relationship with it? Probably not. But in order to prove myself to the other men in this world, I do what I have to.

Including putting my dating life to the side.

It's what vibrators are for, right?

"You would help me?"

"If you want me to, yes."

"Fuck," Nick groans, leaning back in his chair. "I don't want to say yes."

"Why not? It's not like you have feelings for me to make things messy." I'm blunt. Straight to the point. I don't have time to beat around the bush. "You can help me figure out why I keep scaring off the men I try to date."

"N-n-no," he stammers. "But…it's weird, right? You run the team."

"And it's my job to help my players."

"With dating advice?"

I waggle my head back and forth. "More like tips. To make things easier on you. So maybe you can get—"

"Fifteen minutes out of a date?" Nick interrupts.

I snort out a very unladylike laugh. "You said it, not me."

Nick laughs with me. "We were both thinking it."

"I was not."

"Were too," Nick fires back. "I'm a walking disaster."

"You are full of confidence on the ice."

"Hockey I know. Women? It's a whole different ball game, if you will."

"We're not that scary," I tell him, smiling.

"You're not? Seems it to me."

"Then let me help you."

I don't know why I'm pushing this. Maybe it's because I watched this date go off the rails, but there's something sweet about the man sitting in front of me. So confident on the ice, but shy and awkward now.

It's hard to figure him out. Could that be part of the allure? The reason I want to do this?

"And it's not a conflict of interest?"

I shrug a shoulder at his question. "It's not like we're dating. A few tips here and there for both of us. Get us through the hard part so we can each find a date…"

"Who's not an influencer. At least for me."

I shake my head. "Who set you up on this date?"

"The guys did. Well, Piper too. But yeah."

"Easy for them since they're all partnered off."

"Not Noah. He's focusing on recovering," Nick corrects me.

"I'm hoping he gets back to where he was. A busted knee is never an easy recovery."

It was a hard hit to watch. By no means vicious, but the hit Graham Fisher leveled on our star player took him out for a few months. The road to recovery has been longer than anyone wants. Having to move your star center to the third line to limit his playing time? Not an easy thing to do.

"He'll get there. No one is more committed to the team than he is."

I throw my hands up, nearly knocking into a passing waiter. "I'm not saying that. Just saying it's hard."

"Hey, I did it."

"You did." Of course, Nick's injury wasn't as severe. He was only out a few weeks. But the fact that Nick is talking to me in full sentences, without stammering? I'll take it. "We need our goalie now more than ever."

"It's going to be a hard few weeks ahead of us."

"You'll manage."

"Even if I have you teaching me the ropes in the meantime?" Nick quirks a brow at me.

It sends a ripple through my belly. Something I haven't felt in a long time. A *very* long time. I ignore it, sipping on my wine.

"I'll have you ready to go in no time."

Nick leans across the table, coming within a few inches of me. Again, there's that ripple, the one I do my best to ignore.

"And you really want me to help you? After witnessing this disaster?"

"Like I said, Nick. You showed up. If you can help me

get someone to show up, maybe it'll turn things around for me."

Nick leans across the table, his blue eyes playful now. "Can I just say that whoever stood you up is insane?"

"That's sweet of you."

"You really want to do this?" Nick asks.

Looking around the bar, it seems like everyone here is coupled up, huddled together over their tables. Usually, it doesn't bother me. Even though I'm thirty-six, I made the decision to put my career first. Now, it seems, it might not have been the best decision. Some days it feels like dating is a whole new thing for me that I've never done before at all.

And now I'm trying to get Nick to help me with this? Maybe I'm out of my mind, but it's not like things can get any worse.

"I wouldn't have suggested it if I didn't want to do it."

Nick holds his glass out to me in cheers. "Then I guess I'd better take you up on your offer."

Chapter Six

NICK

Don't keep me waiting, Nick.

It's the singular thought propelling me forward toward the executive suites the following morning.

I must be crazy to agree to this plan. Having the GM of the team give me dating lessons? And helping her in return?

I've lost my mind.

But after the disaster of a date last week, I need help. When the guys asked how it went, I played it off like it didn't work out between the two of us. I don't need the grief from them. Or them to think I'm some virgin who's never dated before.

The one good thing about Bexley is that she'll be discreet. I know she won't go blabbing everything to everyone she knows.

The glass doors to the C-suites show no one has arrived yet. I'm early, the clock not quite ticking toward seven. The lights are off as computers cast their glow through the empty space. Pictures of the team line the walls as I make my way toward the only office with a light on.

The quiet knock echoes through the empty space.

"Come in."

As I peek my head in the door, Bexley gives me a warm smile. Her office is a direct contrast to her. The woman walks into a room and demands power and attention. Her office? Everything is soft. Warm grays and pinks. A soft white rug under my old black sneakers. Natural wood desk and bookshelves. Awards bestowed upon the team throughout the years grace the shelves. The windows behind her are dark. I know they look out onto the ice where we practice.

"Hey."

I shove my hands in the pocket of my Black Diamonds hoodie, not quite knowing what to do with them.

Bexley stands, coming around the desk. She's shorter today—not in her usual standard-issue uniform of a skirt and heels. Instead, she's in tight black pants and an over-sized cream sweater.

Her dark hair flows around her shoulders. It looks so soft that I want to reach out and touch it.

"I was worried you wouldn't show up today."

"Does that mean I passed the first test?" I cross my arms, almost to protect myself from what's to come.

When Bexley suggested we help each other, I thought I was crazy when I agreed to it. When I gave her my number, I knew I was.

But after the disaster with Caroline, I knew I needed help. Especially if I want what the guys have.

"Showing up is always the hard part on a first date."

"Don't I know it."

Bexley motions toward the oversized love seat that takes up the right side of her office.

"I'd show up for you, Nick," Bexley tells me.

Why does that do funny things to my insides?

"Y-you would?" I stutter out.

She nods, resting her chin in her hand on the back of the love seat. "And that's saying a lot, because I've canceled and been stood up. A lot."

"Who would stand you up?" I blurt out. "You're gorgeous."

Why the hell do I keep saying this out loud?

She gives me a warm smile, but sidesteps my awkward comment. "This"—she waves a hand around her office—"can be rather intimidating to a guy."

Dropping down onto the couch next to her, I try to settle the nerves clanking around in my stomach.

It's weird, being with her like this. Her feet are bare—toenails painted a deep-red color. She's relaxed, comfortable like this.

Again, messing with my image of her.

"I thought guys like women who like sports."

"It's almost too much in my case. And I don't know how to turn it off," Bexley confesses.

I laugh. "And you want my help? Hockey is my life, too, you know."

Bexley laughs back, and it's a warm and sweet sound. Something I want to hear more of. "Maybe I didn't quite think this through then."

"Meanwhile, I'd be okay finding someone who doesn't want anything to do with hockey."

"Why's that?" Bexley shifts on the couch, her knee pressing into my thigh. Her perfume—something sweet, cotton candy maybe?—wafts over me. It's heavenly.

"I think this life can be a lot for anyone. My sister grew up the same as I did, seeing my dad leave for away games, and even now, it can be hard on her. The long road trips can be taxing on anyone."

"It can be intimidating." Bexley nods, knowing exactly what I'm talking about. "It's not for the faint of heart."

"Even my college girlfriend hated it, and that wasn't nearly as bad."

"Did you know my college boyfriend played hockey? I don't think I minded him being gone because it gave me a chance to hang out with my girlfriends."

"Maybe that's your first problem." I scrub a nervous hand across the back of my neck. "Not that you need me to point that out."

Bexley gives me a playful smile. "Wanting to hang out with friends over guys? Nothing new there. Now it's just work over wanting to date."

"I guess we both have that in common."

"Two peas in a pod."

My eyes continue to stay focused on Bexley as she talks about work. Listening to her is mesmerizing. I could sit here and listen to her talk for hours. There's something about the smooth cadence of her voice that sets me at ease.

I've never felt like this with anyone, so why am I feeling it with Bexley? With the one person I shouldn't be feeling these things with?

"You know," I cut in, "I don't think it's a bad thing you focus on work when you're so passionate about it."

"That's one way to put it."

"I'm serious," I tell her. "You're great at your job, and I don't think you should shy away from that. If some guy can't handle that, then he isn't the guy for you."

"Thanks, Nick." Bexley reaches over and squeezes my forearm. It sends a rush of tingles through me. That's new. And not an entirely unwanted feeling. She checks the time, and a sad look comes over her face. "I have a meeting at nine that I need to prep for."

Glancing at my watch, I see how much time has flown by. "I should probably hit the weight room before practice today."

Bexley points a finger at me. "I want my goalie in top shape for this season, so get to it."

"On it, boss." I laugh.

"You know,"—Bexley stands, leading me to the door in her office—"there is one plus side."

"What's that?"

"I hate to point it out, but you're talking to me without hesitation."

I shrug. "It's easy to talk hockey."

"And here we are supposed to be branching out from sports."

Bexley's laughter rings out in her office, and it makes me want to keep making her do it. I shouldn't be so taken with this woman. We're helping each other.

"Listen, why don't you come over to my house next

week? I know this whole thing might seem weird, but maybe figuring out how to help each other date other people might be easier if we're not here."

"Okay."

I answer without any hesitation. I want more of Bexley. More of this side of her. I don't know how I'm helping her, but if that's the guise we're both going with, I'll keep playing along.

Because I'm not ready to give up Bexley.

Not when I only just got her.

Chapter Seven

NICK

This is going to be a lot harder than I thought.

After Bexley told me to come to her house, she texted me her address. I shouldn't be surprised that she lives in one of the nicest parts of Denver. I drive through the neighborhood, taking note of the tree-lined streets with high fences that block the houses from view.

When I spot her address, I notice that Bexley's house is more modest than I thought it would be. It's an old brick house with black shutters and perfectly manicured flower beds out front.

Parking in the circular drive, I put the car in park and try to steady my nerves. I know this is better than meeting at the office—fewer prying eyes—but it's a weird feeling to be at her house.

At my general manager's house.

For dating lessons. *Mutual* dating lessons.

Yeah, I don't think this is going to get any less weird.

Summoning up what energy I still have after a tough practice, I head toward her front door and give a knock that sounds more confident than I feel.

I know that confidence was one of the things Bexley told me to have, but it's hard. Hard not to convince myself that any woman I'm going to find will only want me for the material things I have.

My position as the starting goalie for the Black Diamonds and the money that comes with it.

When Bexley opens the door, a weird fluttery feeling I haven't felt in a long time settles in my gut.

She's in a curve-hugging tank top and a pair of running shorts. All that hair is pulled into a wild bun on top of her head, and her feet are bare. Her face has no hint of makeup on it.

It's a contrast to how I've always seen her. Bexley never looks less than perfect at the office. Maybe it's her wall she puts up for the world to see. The wall she puts up when she tries to date.

This is a completely different woman than I'm used to.

"Hey. Did you find the place okay?" she asks. Her smile is wide and welcoming as she throws her arm out to usher me inside.

"Uh, yeah."

It's hard not to stare at how nice her house is. Everything is perfectly in its place.

Two large sofas sit facing each other in front of a stone fireplace, the focal point in the room. A vase with fresh flowers sits on the mantel. Old time hockey pictures line the gray walls mixed in with pictures of family. A set of stairs is off to one side before it opens to the kitchen, which is all white and marble with stainless steel appliances.

It's soft, yet hard at the same time.

Kind of like Bexley, I'm learning.

"You want anything to drink?" she asks, breaking me out of my perusal of her house.

The windows at the back of the house open up to a

small yard that leads out to a creek. It's like her own little oasis in the middle of the city.

"Uh, I'll just do water."

"You sure you don't want anything stronger? I know I could use it." She smirks at me.

"Well, I'll have whatever you're having then." I give her a smile back

"Agreeable. First thing a woman likes in a man."

"Really?"

Bexley's laughter is warm and playful. "Nick, you can have whatever you want to drink. It makes no difference to me."

I laugh at that. "Alright, if you've got a bourbon, I'll take a bourbon."

"Bourbon? That's an interesting choice."

I watch as she strides to a small liquor cabinet and pulls out two glasses and what looks to be an expensive bottle of bourbon.

"Well, it's my dad's drink of choice, so when my sister and I turned twenty-one, he made sure we knew how to drink it and drink it properly."

"I feel like there's more to that story," Bexley says, eyeing me.

I scrub a nervous hand down the back of my neck. Bexley picks up on my nerves immediately.

"Since we're here to get to know each other and figure this whole dating thing out together, why don't you tell me more?"

"Aren't you just diving right into the deep end?"

Bexley grabs two square ice cubes from the freezer for our glasses and then pours a hearty sample of the amber liquid into each one, before passing mine over.

"Well, what better way to cut all the awkwardness than to just go for it?"

That's one way of putting it.

Bexley holds out her glass, and I clink my glass to hers and take a fortifying sip.

Damn, that feels good. The burn of it sliding down my throat. It helps to calm the anxious nerves that I'm feeling.

"Is it okay to say that I'm weirded out by this?" I confess.

She smiles, leaning across the counter.

I do everything I can not to ogle the gentle slope of her neck, the way it gives way toward her chest.

Fuck, Bexley really is a stunning woman.

"I'd be more weirded out if you weren't weirded out," she agrees. "We're in this together. I need help, you need help. We can make it work."

"We can make it work," I parrot back to her.

"Okay, back to this whole 'your dad got you drinking bourbon on your twenty-first birthday' thing."

I smile. Talking about my family is easy. This I can do.

"I've never been much of a drinker, but when the situation calls for it, he wanted me to have something to go to, and bourbon was always his drink of choice. I think it was his way of wanting to bond with me."

"Are you not close with him?" Bexley asks.

"I am, but I'm more like my pops. Quiet and shy."

Bexley studies me, and I do what I can not to squirm under her stare. Her eyes are forceful as she takes me in.

"It's interesting because you're not that way on the ice."

"Really?"

She shakes her head. "You're confident. Like you own that six feet of space between the posts on the ice, and no one is going to get in it but you."

Damn. Bexley sure knows how to make a guy feel good.

"It's easier on the ice for me. I can block everything out and focus on the game. It's the outside noise that gets me."

"C'mon."

Grabbing my hand—while I do my best to ignore the rumble of heat that blazes through me—Bexley leads me to her living room and pulls me down onto the couch next to her.

"Sorry, it's better if we talk in here," she tells me. "You know, I never saw your dad play, but it sounds like you take after him too."

I swirl the liquid in my drink before taking another sip. "Even though football and hockey are so different, he taught me a lot of how to carry myself when I play."

"It's what makes you a GM's dream." Bexley swirls her finger around the rim of her glass and it's intoxicating—watching the way it moves.

I wish she was doing it on certain parts of me, to be honest.

Fuck. That's not what this is, Nick. Stop thinking with your lower brain and use your actual brain.

"I'm glad you think so. I never want to get caught up in the lifestyle that seems to suck in a lot of guys. One of the best lessons Dad taught me."

Bexley drops her elbow onto the back of the couch and rests her cheek on her fist there.

"How did you get into hockey over football? Were you a *massive* disappointment to him?"

That gets a hearty laugh out of me. "Noah was actually the one to convince me to play hockey."

"Really?"

I nod. "He was the oldest out of my dads' group of friends' kids, and when I realized he was cool, I wanted to do what he did."

A syrupy-sweet smile washes over Bexley's face. All I

want to do is keep it there. To keep her looking at me like that.

Is that bad? I shouldn't be wanting that from her. It's not what this is.

"That's adorable, Nick."

"As soon as he started, everyone kind of followed. If one kid wanted to do something, they signed us all up. I think they did it so they could stay friends, but they're as close as ever."

A weird look washes over Bexley's face when I say that. Maybe her dad is a sore subject for her? Shit. This is why I'm so bad at dating. I never know what to say or what is going to make things awkward.

Instead, I keep blubbering on trying to make it better. Or worse. I don't really know at this point.

"I didn't really pick up hockey until high school. Once I hit my growth spurt, I realized I could play well, and it shut up the kids at my school. It was a lifesaver for me."

"What do you mean, lifesaver?"

I blow out a breath. "It's not something I really like talking about…"

Bexley reaches over and squeezes my forearm. Again, ignoring how good her touch feels, my eyes connect with hers. "You don't have to tell me. But if you want to, it'll stay between us."

I believe her. It's not something I feel often, but with Bexley? I do. She makes it easy to trust her. Whether it's because she grew up the daughter of a hockey player or the fact that she manages the team, Bexley is someone I want to open up to.

"Middle school and high school weren't exactly easy for a shy kid like me. Growing up with a dad who was recognized everywhere in Denver made it hard. People always coming up to us and wanting autographs or pictures. I hated the attention. And then kids thought I was being a snob and not wanting to talk to them when really, I just hated being the center of attention."

Bexley listens to every word, not interrupting, giving me the space to tell her about my childhood.

"I was bullied a lot because of it, but when I started playing hockey, suddenly everyone wanted to be my friend."

"Nick, I'm so sorry," Bexley whispers.

"I think it's part of why I'm so bad at all of this." I wave a hand around in the air. "Dating. Trying to connect with people."

"Because you think there's an ulterior motive from them?"

"Exactly. My formative years weren't easy, and it makes it hard for me to really trust people."

Even though I trusted Bexley the minute she sat down at my table.

"Did your dads try and help?"

"They did. But they can't control everything. It's why I'm so close with my family. I spent more time with them than anyone else."

Bexley sighs, sinking back into the cushions of the couch. "I didn't have that."

"Really?" I sip my drink, ice cube clinking around inside as I drain the last finger.

"My dad was a completely different person after my mom died. It changed him. It's like he didn't know what to do with me, so he put everything he had into hockey. For me to get any kind of attention from him, I learned everything I could about the sport just to try and impress him."

"I had no idea."

Bexley looks sad, and I wish I could take away her pain with the wave of a wand, but I can't.

"And once he handed over the reins of the team to me, he flitted off to Europe. It's just been me here with the team ever since."

"Hey." This time, it's me giving her arm a reassuring squeeze. "You're killing it. I mean, hell, we won the cup last year. That's not an easy feat."

"God. All we're talking about is sports." Bexley laughs, breaking the mood between the two of us. "You see why I have so much trouble with this."

"How are you not someone's dream girl?"

Bexley's eyes widen ever so slightly.

Fuck.

"See, this is why I'm terrible at this. I never know the right thing to say." Setting my glass on the table, I bury my face—burning bright with embarrassment—in my hands.

"Hey, stop overthinking it. You agreed to this whole thing. To helping one another get better."

I feel movement next to me, and when I turn, Bexley is right there. Not even an inch away from me.

This close, I can see every detail of her beautiful face.

The way her lashes kiss her cheeks. The slight upturn at the tip of her nose. How her bottom lip sticks out ever so slightly more than her top lip.

Pale, flawless skin.

It would be so easy to capture her lips with mine. To taste the sweet and smoky bourbon on her lips. To feel how soft they really are.

Would it be as good as I'm imagining? A woman like Bexley has to be a good kisser. Not good—fucking great.

Bexley's nails claw into my arm, drawing me out of my daydreaming.

"I think we should call it a day."

It's like a bucket of ice water thrown on me.

Clearing my throat, I stand and try to put as much

distance between the two of us as I can. I don't need her to think that I'm some kid who can't keep it in his pants.

Of course that's probably how she sees me. She's more than a fucking decade older than I am. God, she's probably taking pity on me. I should end this before I get sucked into her world even further.

"Maybe you can come over next week?"

"Sure thing, Bexley." So much for ending this.

"Bex. Call me Bex."

I smile down at her. "Okay, Bex."

But when she shows me to the door and leans up to press a kiss to my cheek, all thought flees.

"I'll see you soon, okay?" she tells me.

"Not soon enough," I mutter.

Chapter Eight

NICK

"I think he's sick."

"Can you take him to the vet?" Piper asks over the phone.

She's the only person I could think to call since her brother is deciding not to pick up the phone. Not that Noah can't have a life, but it's not like I know what to do when Oreo isn't eating.

"It's almost eight, Piper. The vet isn't open."

"There has to be an emergency vet in Denver you can go to."

"Do you think I should? Is that not being dramatic? Maybe I can just wait until tomorrow."

"Nick." There's a force behind her words. One that means I should listen to whatever she's telling me. "Oreo can't tell you what he's feeling, so go to the vet. It's not dramatic to go tonight. Besides, what if it gets worse and then how will you feel tomorrow?"

"Way to call me out," I mutter.

"You're being ridiculous, Nick," she tells me. I can hear the exasperation in her voice. "Your vet will not think anything of you for bringing him in. I would do the same thing for Puck without hesitation. He'll probably talk your ear off about how great your game was the other night."

I smile at her as I stroke Oreo's soft fur between his ears. "I guess."

"Keep me posted on how it goes."

"Sure thing."

I end the call and scoop the small ball of fur into my arms. As much as I don't want to get shamed by taking him in, I'd rather do it and worry about that later.

Even if it means I'll have to bail on Bex tonight. We haven't hung out that often, but I love the time we do spend together. Maybe a little too much.

NICK

Sorry, I won't be able to make it tonight. Oreo isn't feeling well and I need to take him to the vet. Which seems dramatic because he's a bunny, right? Do bunnies even get sick? I don't know, and now I'm worried that if I wait until tomorrow, something bad will happen, so I'm taking him in and won't be over tonight. Sorry.

I DON'T THINK TWICE BEFORE HITTING send on the verbal diarrhea I just spewed out at her. I find the closest emergency vet—only two in the Denver area take bunnies —and give them a call, telling the nurse about Oreo's ailments. Getting confirmation to take him in, I put him in his carrier and head that way.

Even with it being post-rush hour, traffic is still a bitch through the city. It's a slow crawl until I finally make it to the twenty-four-hour vet that's situated next to a diner and a nail salon in a strip mall.

The glass bell over the door tinkles as I pull it open. A nurse in scrubs is sitting at the desk typing away on the computer. The lobby has the usual antiseptic smell of a vet's office.

"Hi. How can I help you?" she asks by way of greeting.

"I called a little while ago about my bunny."

"Oreo, yes." Her hazel eyes light up in recognition. "I need you to fill out a few forms while you wait, and the doctor will see you shortly. If you'd like to come back, I can get you in a room."

"Thank you."

I follow her through the hallways that are covered with pictures of happy animals and different types of medications for them. The overhead lights are bright as she shows me to a small room.

"You can set Oreo up here and we'll see him soon."

I give her a nod before she's out the door on the other side of the room. Setting Oreo's carrier on the table, I peer in at him before starting on the stack of forms. "It's okay, buddy. You'll be feeling better in no time."

I don't know if I'm saying it more to reassure him or myself. Opening the door to the carrier, I take him in my arms and stroke his soft fur.

Was getting a pet bunny on my list of things to do my first season as an NHL player? Hell no. But when I saw him, I couldn't pass him up. Oreo doesn't care what kind of game I have, good or bad. It's someone that doesn't judge me and that is why I like having him in my life. A calm from the chaos of everything else going on.

"Mr. Brooks-Young. Wow. I didn't believe it when the nurse told me who was here." The door in the back of the room opens and the vet pops in. He's an older man with dyed brown hair and a goatee. A stethoscope hangs around his neck. A dog and cat are embroidered on his navy scrubs.

"Umm, hi."

"Sorry." He waves his hand in front of him. "Dr. Gray. I didn't mean to come in like that. I'm a lifelong Black Diamonds fan, so crazy to think you're here. But let's get the patient taken care of."

"I appreciate it."

The vet takes him from my arms and looks him over. He asks me questions—about Oreo and hockey—as he examines him. I do my best not to fidget in the hard plastic chair.

"It looks like he has a bit of a temperature," he tells me.

"Will you be able to treat that?" I ask.

He nods. "Of course. Bunnies get sick just like the rest of us, so I'm glad you brought him in. I'll have our nurse get you some meds, and he should perk up in a few days."

"Thanks for not making me feel stupid," I tell him, taking Oreo back into my arms.

"Pets are our family. I have two dogs, three cats, and my own bunny at home. Believe me, I get it."

I smile at him. "That's way more than I could ever manage."

"I guess not with your schedule." He sticks his hand out for me to shake. "We'll get you the oral prescription, and it should be cleared up in a few days. If he's still lethargic, you can take him to your regular vet to follow up. And listen, you keep up the good work. I'd like another trophy brought home."

I blow out the breath I've been holding. "I'll try, thanks. And I really appreciate you fitting us in tonight."

"It's why we're here." He gives me a warm smile before heading out the door he came through.

"See? All's okay, Oreo." I squat down to look him in the eyes. He doesn't understand a word I'm saying, but it's more to put me at ease than anything else.

I don't know how parents handle sick kids when I'm this worked up over my pet rabbit.

"Okay, Mr. Brooks-Young. Five milliliters twice a day for a week and that should have Oreo feeling better in no time." The nurse enters the room and hands me a white bag. "Your wife is waiting for you outside."

"Wife?" I grab the white bag and scoot Oreo back into his carrier.

I follow her out the door I came in, wondering who on earth is here. Piper didn't come, did she?

But when the door to the waiting area opens, I draw up short.

"Bexley?"

A Black Diamonds cap hides her face, but I'd recognize her anywhere. She's wearing a black jacket over a plain white T-shirt and joggers.

What in the world is she doing here?

"Mr. Brooks-Young?"

"Sorry." I shake off the stupor of seeing Bexley and pay for the office visit before following her outside.

"How's Oreo?" Bex asks. It's dark now, the only light coming from the office behind us and the diner next door. The parking lot lights don't really shine much next to the building.

"What are you doing here?" I ask her by way of answer.

She smiles up at me. "You sounded worried."

"In a text?"

"You rambled."

Fuck me. Of course I did. "Sorry, I guess I was more worried than I thought."

"You have a bunny?" she asks, crossing her arms.

"I do."

"And is he doing okay?"

I hold up the carrier, as if she can see him, but it's too dark out here. "A bit of a temperature, but other than that, he should be okay."

Bex assesses me, almost as if debating what to say next. "Want to grab something to eat?" She nods to the diner behind us.

"I don't think he's allowed in."

"Doesn't matter. We can eat in my car." The car behind me beeps. "Get Oreo situated and I'll grab us something to eat."

I don't have time to answer before she's pushing open the door to the diner and striding up to the counter.

"I guess we're having dinner with her," I tell Oreo.

Opening the door to Bexley's SUV, I get in the front seat, turn on the lights, and pull Oreo out of his carrier. By the time I give him a dose of the meds and get him curled up in his blanket, Bexley is opening the door with the greasiest-smelling food imaginable.

And it smells fucking delicious. "I got a little bit of everything."

"It smells great."

Bex sets two milkshakes in the cupholders and pulls out a burger, chicken fingers, a patty melt, and fries.

"I might have gone overboard." Bex laughs. "I didn't know what you'd want."

Now that I'm not as worried about Oreo, I'm starving. "This is great."

I grab a few fries and take a bite of a chicken tender.

"How did I not know you have a bunny?" Bex asks,

picking up the patty melt and taking a bite. "Cassie would have a field day with you if she knew."

I smile back at her, dunking a chicken finger into the ketchup cup she brought with her. "And that's exactly the reason I haven't told anyone about him. I don't think he'd like the attention."

Bex quirks a brow at me and sets her sandwich down. "He wouldn't, or you wouldn't?"

"Am I that easy to read?"

"Yes." She holds her hands out. "Can I hold him?"

"Just be gentle," I tell her as I pass him off to her. Bex sets Oreo in her lap and rubs the fur between his ears.

"You're cute," she tells him.

God, how I wish she were talking to me. The smile that sits on her face is one of pure adoration. It's how everyone looks at Oreo. How can you not? He's fucking adorable.

"Everyone loves him."

"I can see why." Her eyes flit up to mine. The low light in the car catches them and it does more funny things to my insides.

Maybe I need to see a doctor. I shouldn't be having these kinds of reactions to a woman looking at me. Especially not Bexley.

I shouldn't be as taken with her as I am.

"He's pretty much always this cute. Except when he's eating. Then he's really fucking cute."

"Okay, you need to bring him over the next time you come."

"Maybe I should just start bringing him on dates."

Bexley laughs, warm and bright, before going back to her meal. "I think that's one way of breaking the ice."

"But..." I grab a fry and swipe it through ketchup before chomping down on it.

"But then would they like you for you, or for your bunny?"

"Touché."

This is easy. Sitting here and talking with her about anything and everything. Eating diner food in her car.

I don't even realize how close we've gotten, both of us leaning across the center console toward each other.

I want to reach out and trace the cupid's bow of her lips. See how she tastes.

Fuck.

Why can't it always be like this?

There's no front either of us are putting on. It's only us. What you see is what you get. Maybe this is why it's so hard for us? People expect us to be entirely different people than who we really are.

The buzzing in my pocket startles me back to reality.

I don't realize how late it's gotten until I glance at the clock on the dash.

"I should probably get going," I tell her.

She looks at the clock and sees that it's well past eleven. Bex gets Oreo back into his carrier, then gets out and meets me by my car.

"Sorry, I didn't realize how late it was. I know you have early practice."

"I've done it on less sleep." If it meant I got to stay here with her all night, I'd happily walk into practice in the same clothes I left in.

"Well, in that case, I'm not sorry for keeping you out late."

"No, you can blame Oreo for that." I laugh.

That draws laughter out of her. "Blame Oreo? I could never."

She shoots me a wink before walking around the hood of her car back to her side.

"Hey Bex?"

I'm not ready for this night with her to end. I want to draw out every last second with her that I can. Even if it's in a quiet, deserted parking lot.

"Yeah?" She stops and spins around.

"Thanks for coming here tonight."

It's weird. I've never really had another person other than family I can count on. Sure, I have the guys. But with all of them starting to couple off, it's made my single status feel like a bigger thing than it should be. Hence the need for them to set me up.

Piper is there for me too, but she has her own life now, and I never want to impose on her.

I want Bex to be someone I can count on. I want to tell her all that, but I've already spewed enough on her tonight.

It looks like she wants to tell me something. Like she has more to say. Instead, she stuffs her hands in her pockets and walks back toward her car.

"Night, Nick."

"Night."

Chapter Nine

BEXLEY

Does Bexley Hart have what it takes to lead this team? The old GM set her up perfectly to win the cup last year, but with the continued spiral of star Noah Fields, the GM needs to step up and take action with this team.

F uck me.

Another day, another article about how it's my fault our star player isn't holding his own. It's not like I make the coaching decisions. Sure, I talk with Coach Barney daily, but I can only do so much. If I cut Noah now, the fans—and press—would have my head. There's no winning in this position.

The knock on my door has me locking my phone and trying to push the article out of my head.

When I open the door, there he is.

Nick.

In a Black Diamonds tee that stretches across his impressive chest and a pair of jeans, he shouldn't look as good as he does.

It's almost criminal how sexy this man is.

"Hey, Bex."

The timbre of his voice does nothing to help cool the feelings that he stirs up in me.

"Hi. How's Oreo doing?" I ask as he brushes past me, leaving his shoes near the front door. He smells clean, like the soap he uses. It sends tingles rushing through my veins.

Stop it, Bex. No feelings for this guy. You're helping each other.

"Much better. Hopping around like he was never sick."

"I can't imagine how cute he is," I tell him, leading him toward my dining room.

"He really is." Nick stops short when he sees everything spread out across the wooden table. "Gardening?"

"I take it this isn't something you've done before?" I laugh, walking over to one of the large, ceramic pots.

"Can't say that I have."

"Remember, shared interests."

"And how is this supposed to help you?"

I grab the trowel and hand it over to him. "Because it makes me more approachable. Less 'all about hockey' and more relatable, I guess."

Nick laughs. Warm and smooth, it sends funny feelings to my insides. "You're only guessing about that?"

I shrug a shoulder. My sweater falls over it, and I don't miss the way Nick's eyes catch on the exposed skin there.

"I don't know why a woman loving hockey is so intimidating to them. Are they afraid I'm going to try and show them up with everything I know?"

Nick nods. "That's exactly it."

I roll my eyes. "I don't feel like I should have to make myself smaller to impress them."

"I didn't say that," Nick corrects, taking a step closer to me. His sock-clad feet graze my bare toes. There's something so intimate about it, that I have to look away to try and find relief for everything he's making me feel. "You're a smart and powerful woman, Bex. You shouldn't try and change yourself for anyone."

Why couldn't Nick be my date for tomorrow? I know this is what we agreed to. To each schedule a date and see how it goes. But it's not what I want now. Not after I've gotten to know Nick more.

"You're going to help me repot some of my plants." I steer the conversation back to safe ground.

"Some?" Nick's eyes are wide as he takes in the various plants littering my entire dining room table. "This is more than some, Bex."

"Well, they're getting too big for their pots and they need more space."

"Are you sure you trust me? I'm pretty sure I have a black thumb."

"If they die, I'll send you an invoice." I laugh.

"What do I need to do?"

I give Nick instructions on moving the plants from one pot to another, and watch as he transfers the first one. "You're good at this," I tell him.

"My pops is a teacher. If I didn't pay attention, he would've grounded me."

I bark out a laugh at that, tending to my own red ruby plant. "I can't even imagine you not paying attention."

Nick gives me a sly smile. "I was always the Goody-Two-Shoes in class because of it. I never wanted to misbehave and draw attention to myself."

"I can only imagine how sweet you were back then."

Being with Nick like this is easy. Too easy. Watching him as he works is mesmerizing. The way his hands dig into the soil. The strength in them. How long and perfectly thick his fingers are.

I wonder what they'd feel like inside of me?

God, who knew gardening could be such a turn-on?

"Why gardening?" Nick asks, pulling my attention away from his hands and the dirty spiraling of my thoughts.

I blow out a breath. "My mom loved it. It's one of the things I still do to keep her close. It helps me turn my brain off when I come home. If I don't spend all my time with them, they aren't going to fault me."

"You talk like they're people."

I run a thumb and forefinger over the green and white leaves of the snow queen plant in front of me. It was always one of her favorites, and I love having it around. Almost like it's a piece of her here with me.

"I like to think they all have certain personalities. My mom seemed to think so."

"You miss her."

I nod, not looking at Nick. "I do."

It's a well-known fact that my mother died when I was young. It seems every time a news story is done on me, they highlight that part of my life. How it shaped me into the woman I am now.

It's hard to talk about it sometimes, losing her to a sudden illness when I was so young. Even now, with Nick here, I want to tell him, but I don't feel like I can open up that part of me. Not without carving out my heart.

Nick's hand closes over mine. Shifting my attention, I see his eyes are on me. Only a few inches of space separate the two of us.

I can see dark brown specks in those blue eyes of his. A small smattering of freckles on his cheeks. The one curl of hair that falls over his forehead.

It sends a multitude of different sensations through me now, pushing out the feelings of sadness.

Desire.

Heat.

Want.

I ache in the best way for this man. This man that is off-limits because he's my player and over a decade younger than I am.

Is it against the rules? No. But in the court of public opinion, it wouldn't matter. The optics would be terrible for the team.

The team is my life, and it has to come first.

Always.

Shaking his hand off, I clear all these thoughts I shouldn't be having. His own eyes are serious, staring at me. Studying me.

Could he be feeling this too?

No, Bex.

I need to get this night back onto safer ground. Somewhere that isn't the thought of Nick and me touching. Kissing. Giving in to what we're both feeling, if his reaction is anything to go on.

"Are you ready for your date tomorrow?"

Whatever we were feeling, I snuffed it out with that one question. Nick settles back onto his heels, staring down at his hands.

"I guess so."

"No," I correct him. "You are. She's a teacher, right?"

"She is." Nick looks up at me, and I hate the look in his eyes. It feels like he really doesn't want to do this, but knows it's for the best.

Hell, the last thing I want to be doing is going out with my planned date, but it is what it is.

"You'll do great. Plenty in common to talk about."

"And if I turn into a bumbling idiot?"

"You won't. And if you get nervous, just take a few deep breaths."

"I don't know why I'm not like that with you."

I give him a reassuring smile. "It's because you've gotten to know me. Pretend like you already know them so you have the confidence you do right now."

"Confidence. Okay."

I can see him psyching himself up, telling himself to have confidence. It's such a contrast from the man I've gotten to know these last few weeks.

Nick is full of confidence on the ice. Like he knows he's going to stop whatever comes his way. Off the ice is a completely different story.

But now that I know him, I can see his confidence in the little things he does. He doesn't have to exude it all the time. It's in the small touches. His words. His actions.

Nick Brooks-Young might be the most enticing, confident man I've ever met. And I have no hold on him.

"Listen, you should probably get going. I've got early meetings tomorrow."

And if you stay any longer, I don't know what I'll do. Invite him to stay? Sleep in my bed? A quick fuck to try and get these feelings out of my system?

"Sure." Nick stands, heading to the sink to wash his hands. "And hey, good luck on your date tomorrow too."

"Thanks."

Shutting the door, I collapse back against it. Everything is telling me this is a mistake. Going out with someone else tomorrow doesn't feel right. But I agreed to this with Nick. *For* Nick.

Except now, he's the only person I want.

Maybe I need a lesson in how not to fall for my player.

Chapter Ten

NICK

Ready for our date?

Our date? Don't you mean dates?

Fine, yes. Are you ready?

Will it make a difference if I'm not?

We've talked about this. You'll be fine.
Didn't you say Angie knows her from work?

Yes, but I don't have a lot of faith in this
after the first disaster

Not the right attitude to have going into this

And what would the right attitude be?

Be positive. Remember, don't be someone
other than yourself

Even if I turn into a bumbling idiot like last
time?

You won't, I promise.

You have a lot of faith in me

It's because I know you can do it

Thanks. Are you ready?

Eh, as ready as I'll ever be

That's not the right attitude to have either

Well, what can I say? I'm not getting great vibes off this guy, but we'll see

Why aren't you vibing with him?

Just doesn't feel like there's any chemistry there

How can you know until you meet him? Give the guy a chance

I am. But, confession…he told me something

Yeah? What is it?

He doesn't like hockey

…

Right?

How can he not like hockey? Does he know what you do?

I told him I manage a team

Not exactly a lie, but not the whole truth

He told me he can't follow the puck and doesn't enjoy the game

Doesn't enjoy the game? I'm...at a loss

Right? The only reason I'm giving this guy a chance is because we made a deal to each go on a date

I would fully support you backing out. Not liking hockey? I can't imagine. That'd be like not liking football.

Hey, you got me liking that now too

Maybe you'll love two sports now. Does this guy like football?

I didn't ask. I couldn't get past him not liking hockey

Well, this could be an epic disaster for both of us

Well, when you put it like that...

I'm not really being positive about this. It could be the best date of my life!

That's the spirit

<<side eye emoji>>

Nick! C'mon. I'm serious. We need to make this work

I'll try. I promise.

Promise, promise?

I said yes, didn't I?

> Okay, fine. I guess. Good luck and I'll see you tomorrow?

> You too

I hate this. I one hundred percent hate this.

I'm on a date with someone Angie knows from work. My sister all but guaranteed that she and I would hit it off. She's a teacher—something I want to do after hockey, so why wouldn't we work well?

Except this whole thing feels off.

I don't want to be on this date with just any woman.

The only person I want sitting across the table from me is Bex. When did that happen? When did I start thinking—and feeling—more for her? I'm not exactly sure, but it's a feeling I wish I could give in to.

Both of us coming to the same restaurant where I had my last failed date doesn't feel like a great idea now. It's not like we're going to be able to critique what we're doing in real time. Now it feels like I'm going to be staring at her the entire time, wondering how it's going instead of focusing on my own date.

But it's just as dark in here as before, which means that hopefully not everyone can see how this date goes. Speaking of, based on the time, my date should be here by now.

It's not filling me with the warm fuzzies that she's not here yet.

As I look over at the door of the restaurant, the woman I really want to see is here.

Bex.

Holy shit. She looks fucking sexy as hell, in a dark,

skin-tight black skirt and a white sweater to show off her curves. The guy she's meeting is one lucky bastard. Bex's dark hair curls down around her back, and her face is expertly done up.

Does she even realize the effect she has on me?

Her eyes sweep the restaurant, landing briefly on me and shooting me a small, knowing smile. When they land on someone else, I spot the man she's meeting.

Dark brown hair, perfectly neat, with a smile aimed directly at her. He's dressed in a finely pressed suit. He looks like the exact type of person who Bex would like.

My date still isn't here, so it's all I can do not to watch Bex like a creep. The way she smiles at him. The way she touches him.

Damn it.

"Nick?"

My eyes snap to the woman standing over me now, with a short, blonde pixie hairstyle, a warm smile, and brown eyes that are staring down at me.

"Edith?" I stand, holding out my hand to her. "Hi. It's nice to meet you."

"It's nice to meet you too."

I gesture for her to take a seat.

"Do you want something to drink?"

"I'm okay with water," she tells me. "I'm a little nervous."

I give her a smile that hopefully relays the same thing. Hopefully it will help set us both at ease. "I am too."

Edith looks shocked at this. "Why? Aren't you some big, bad hockey player?"

I laugh, sinking back into my chair. "Is that what Angie told you about me?"

Her eyes go wide, like I caught her in a lie or something. "I mean, she told me you play hockey. Aren't you all supposed to be cocky players?"

"Then my sister definitely didn't tell you about me."

"You seem pretty suave to me."

"You might be the first person to ever call me suave, Edith," I tell her.

Her eyes cast downward, and she starts picking at her rolled-up napkin. I cut a quick glance at Bex, seeing her eyes on me.

Is she feeling the same way I am? Like she wants to have me sitting across from her and not this perfectly nice person in front of me?

Not that there's anything wrong with Edith, but she's not the woman I want.

"You're a teacher?" I ask her, trying to draw her into starting a conversation.

"I am." She nods, not elaborating any further.

"What grade do you teach?"

"Third."

I guess it's going to be completely on me to carry this conversation tonight. Is it easier because of everything Bex has taught me? Or is it easier because I don't see this going anywhere?

"I want to go into teaching once I retire from the league."

"I need to use the restroom." Edith bolts up from the table, her hands nervously twisting in front of her. "I'll be back."

She grabs her purse and heads that way.

"Okay…"

What in the world is going on tonight? Nothing seems to be working in my favor. Angie told me that Edith was a nice girl she knows from her work at the foundation, but she hasn't said more than a dozen words to me tonight.

Is it really me that can't find a nice woman to carry on a conversation?

My eyes track Bex in the restaurant. Like a lighthouse pulling ships safely into harbor.

Everything she's doing says she's enjoying herself. Leaning into the conversation. Maintaining eye contact. And—fuck—touching his arm.

I swig down the rest of my water. Thank God for practice tomorrow because otherwise I'd be hitting the bourbon.

Although I don't think that'd be strong enough to deal with the feelings I'm having right now.

Bex. On a date. With another man.

Fuck.

This is not something I planned on. We were supposed to be helping each other.

"Sir, excuse me." Our server appears next to me. "Your dinner guest asked me to give you this."

He passes over a small piece of paper and leaves the table.

Sorry, Nick. I can't do this. It's not you, it's me. There is someone else and I don't want to be with someone that isn't him. Please forgive me. - Edith

ARE YOU FUCKING KIDDING ME? I really have the worst luck, and now I'm going to have to tell my sister that her date stood me up.

Do they think the more dates I go on, the more they will somehow boost my confidence? If so, it's not working.

Because I don't want their help now.

All I want is Bex.

Locking eyes with her again, I notice her date isn't there. I want to storm over there, grab her, and pull her from this restaurant and tell her how I'm feeling.

I don't give a shit that we're in the middle of a crowded restaurant and people could see us.

I want Bex. That's the long and short of it.

Tired of planning out every move, I pull out my phone and fire off a text to Bex.

Meet me in the bathroom

I HAVE no idea if she'll come or even answer. But I can't take it any longer. All my feelings are being shaken to the point they're ready to explode like a soda bottle.

I don't recall ever feeling like this. But Bex?

She makes me crazy in the best way possible.

I shouldn't be as worked up about this as I am. Bex and I both agreed that we'd go on dates and then we'd circle back around to see how it went for both of us.

Even the thought of her on a date right now has jealousy boiling inside of me. Which isn't something that's ever happened before.

I don't get jealous.

I guess there's a first time for everything.

I don't know what came over me to text her to meet me in the bathroom. I'm still trying to figure that out.

To what…to talk? To tell her to cut her date short and date me instead?

This is becoming a problem with Bex. I want her, but I don't know how to make this happen. All common sense flies out of my head the minute I'm in the same room as her.

God, she really does have something over me.

A few people walk by and give me a small smile but continue on their way. Hopefully they didn't notice who I am because right now I couldn't stand to talk to another human being other than Bex.

When I spot her walking down the hallway to me, there's a determined look on her face.

"Why did you text me to meet you back here?" she hisses.

I don't answer her. Instead, I grab her hand and pull her into one of the individual, unisex bathrooms in the restaurant, giving us more than enough privacy.

"Because Bex…" I shut the door and lock it behind us.

She leans against the wall and I hover over her.

God, she's stunning. The sexiest woman I've ever met. It's unfair how gorgeous she is. The way her lashes kiss her cheeks as she blinks those big brown doe eyes at me, her plump lips covered in a deep-red lipstick.

Fuck, what I would give to see that lipstick around my cock right now.

"Why am I here, Nick?" she asks again.

"Because…"

"Because is not an answer!" Bex snaps. "I was having a perfectly fine date with that man out there—"

"Perfectly fine?" I interrupt. "You don't deserve perfectly fine."

Bex pushes off the wall, coming within an inch of my face. "Oh yeah, what do I deserve then?"

"You deserve fire."

I slam my mouth down over hers and take what I've been dying to have a taste of since the moment I laid eyes on her.

Chapter Eleven

BEXLEY

Holy shit. Nick is kissing me. God, what a fucking kiss.

Finding the lapels of his jacket, I hold on tight and return the kiss. Because I'm helpless to do anything but return it. The way his tongue strokes mine has heat coiling inside me.

I rub my thighs together to try and appease the feeling that's growing inside me.

When he rips his lips from mine and kisses a trail down my jaw to my neck and nibbles, it's all I can do not to come.

"Nick. Oh my God," I murmur. It comes out as more of a purr.

What is this man doing to me?

Nick's hand slides down and finds my ass, cupping it and pulling me in toward him.

Holy shit…into his very hard cock.

"Oh my God, Nick. We can't do this here."

Nick tugs my earlobe between his teeth. "I don't

fucking care, Bex. I need to have you right now. You've been driving me crazy all night."

"What, like you haven't been doing the exact same to me?"

With every glance of Nick's over to me, it made it harder to focus on my date in front of me. Like I said, he was perfectly nice.

But this? Right here with Nick?

All he's done is kiss me and I'm ready to explode.

I want the fire. I want it to consume me from the inside out.

I want Nick.

"Having to watch you with that woman was hard."

"Why?" Nick pulls back. Lust coats his voice and his pupils are wide with need.

"Because—"

"Because isn't an answer." He smirks.

I pull him closer, his mouth hovering over mine. "Because I wanted it to be me."

A grin slides onto Nick's face. "Then it's a good thing she ditched me."

His words clear the lust-induced fog that's settling into my brain.

"Wait, she left?"

He pulls back and nods at me. "Yeah, she did. She went to the bathroom and never came back. Sent a note out with the server and said there was someone else."

"Shit, Nick, I'm sorry."

"It doesn't matter. I didn't want her anyway."

"Oh yeah? Who did you want then?" I ask.

Based on the reaction he's having right now, I have a feeling I know exactly who it is.

"You, Bex. Only you."

I don't think I've ever kissed a man so quickly. There's something about Nick that has pulled me in.

He's my player. More than a decade younger than me. I don't know how or when it happened, but this man gets me. He understands me.

Right now, as we fight for control of this kiss, none of that matters.

All that matters is the two of us and the passion we're both feeling.

I don't know the last time I've felt this alive.

The Nick I first met at the bar that night? He doesn't exist right now.

In his place is a man who's taking control of this kiss, who's hoisting me into his arms and holding me against the wall as he attacks my mouth with his precision.

Attention.

Care.

Fuck me.

"That was the plan." Nick pulls back with a smile on his face, lips swollen from our kiss.

Oh, crap. Did I say those words out loud?

Nick nips at the tender skin of my neck and I arch into his hold. I feel weightless in his arms.

"Bex. I want to fuck you. *Need* to fuck you. Now."

Sinking my fingers into Nick's hair, I pull his focus to me. This is definitely what I want right now. Having Nick inside of me is the only thing I'm thinking about.

I don't give a shit that we're in the back of a restaurant. That, in truth, my date and I ended things early because we didn't feel the spark. Or that Nick's date ditched him.

All that matters right now is the two of us.

Nick and Bexley.

"Fuck, Nick, I need you."

"It's about damn time, Bex."

Setting me down on my feet, Nick makes careful work of the button and zipper of my skirt. The noise of the restaurant is muted behind us. The only thing I can feel is the pounding of my heart as Nick slides my skirt off me and drops it on the floor next to him.

Nick drops to his knees, and I know the instant he notices the wet spot on my underwear. He strokes one finger over them, and I shudder. A full-body shudder that I want to feel again and again at his hands.

"Oh God, Nick, that feels so good."

Nick presses a kiss to that same spot. "It'll feel even better when it's my cock inside of you. Driving you wild. Making you come."

Who is this man and what has he done with Nick?

These strong, confident words that are coming out… I want to feel every single thing he's giving me right now.

"I want to watch you come. Feel you explode on my cock and watch as you come and then come inside of you."

"Oh God, I want all of that," I moan.

Taking a step back, I watch as Nick undoes his own belt and pants. I'm drooling, practically licking my lips while waiting for him to pull himself out.

As Nick grabs his wallet, I decide I don't want to wait anymore and sink to my knees. Reaching past the waistband of his boxers, I free his leaking dick.

"Fuck, Bexley, what are you doing?"

I give him a sensual smile. "Nick, if you don't know what I'm doing down here, then obviously you need a lesson."

"Oh shit," he murmurs as I take his long, thick cock into my mouth.

Swirling my tongue around the tip, I taste the precum

that's already leaking there. It looks like I wasn't the only one affected by the two of us.

Nick drops the condom he'd been holding in his hand and throws his head back in pleasure as I lick and taste before adding my hands into the mix.

Everything about this is dangerous.

Anyone could come knocking on the door at any minute. But I don't care because the only thing I want is Nick. And damn if I won't have him right now.

"Fuck, Bexley. That feels amazing."

Strong fingers slide through my hair, fisting it there. His moves are gentle as he tugs me up and down his long length.

"Fuck, just like that. Yesss," he hisses.

I flick my tongue under the head of his cock and feel as he thrusts farther inside my mouth.

Oh yeah, he definitely liked that.

This is one lesson I wouldn't mind having with him over and over again—learning what he likes and doesn't like. Exploring with him. Discovering things about him that he doesn't share with anyone else.

I love that I get this side of him.

"Fuck, Bex," Nick growls, "I'm not coming in your mouth the first time."

Sliding off him with a wet pop, I smile up at him.

"Fuck, you look beautiful like this." Nick swipes a thumb over my bottom lip.

"Oh yeah, how do I look?"

"Like you've been sucking my cock like a good little girl."

Shit, those words shouldn't do it for me, but they do. Having Nick heap praise on me makes me want to keep doing this.

Instead, I grab the condom that's on the floor, open it,

and roll it down his length. I shuck off my underwear, letting them join my skirt.

Nick doesn't waste another minute. Hoisting me up to my feet, he pulls my leg up and over his hip before lining his cock up and thrusting inside me in one long push.

"Oh!" I gasp. "Nick, that feels amazing."

"You're so damn sweet, Bex. I'm so happy I finally get to have this pretty little pussy."

"Finally?" I ask him, as he slowly drags himself out before pushing back in.

"Yes, finally." He nods.

"Have you been imagining this?" I ask him.

"Fuck yes," he murmurs into my ear, biting my earlobe and tugging it between his teeth. "You're the only woman I've been imagining. Picturing you like this. You're the only woman I want, Bex."

"Then have me."

I clasp his cheeks in my hands and pull him in for a kiss as he increases his pace.

His free hand moves down between us and plays with my clit. All of the sensations are overwhelming in the best way.

I can't remember the last time I felt this good.

Nick Brooks-Young is about ready to destroy me.

"Come on, Bexley, I know you're there."

"I am. I'm so close," I whisper because I can't do anything else except that.

Each thrust, each stroke of his fingers over my clit tips me over the edge as I stifle my scream.

It feels endless, colors bursting behind my eyes, my toes curling. Every part of my body is shaking as I come for this man. Then I feel him explode into the condom inside me.

"Fuck, fuck," he growls into my neck, nipping and sucking there. "So fucking good, Bex, so fucking good."

He holds me through both of our releases before gently setting me on my feet.

Nick's hair is a mess from my fingers running through it, and I have no doubt mine looks the exact same.

Pulling off the condom and tying it up, he drops it into the trash can before tucking himself away and grabbing a wet paper towel to clean me up.

It's a night and day difference.

The commanding man who just fucked me to within an inch of my life in the bathroom and the tender one that's now cleaning me up after.

When he tosses the paper towel away, I grab his hand and pull him close to me. I press up onto my toes and give him a soft kiss.

Easy, unhurried.

I know we need to get out of here, but I don't want to.

I want to stay wrapped up in this hazy, lust-filled bubble I've created with Nick.

"Holy shit, Bex, that was…"

"I know," I tell him, whispering against his mouth. "I know."

"You know," Nick says, "I don't think this is what I had in mind when we said we were going to have a date tonight."

I smile at him. "I was not planning on this either."

"What do you say? No more dates with other people. You and me?"

Nick's face is blissed-out. Happy. Content. I want to see more of it.

"Yeah, Nick. You and me."

Everyone else be damned.

Chapter Twelve

NICK

"Alright, tell us."

"Tell you what?" I ask Cash.

"Tell us what, he says," Cash parrots back to me. He looks to Noah like I'm an idiot because I have no idea what he's talking about.

"Your date." The duh in Noah's tone is implied.

"You know, I'm beginning to think you guys don't like me."

Troy skates up, spraying ice all over us.

"Asshole," Cash mutters.

"Are we talking about the date last night?" Troy asks, ignoring Cash.

"Nicky thinks we don't like him," Noah tells him.

"Uh-oh. Date didn't go well?" Troy eyes me, like he's trying to figure out what's wrong with me. "Angie said she would love you."

I roll my eyes at him. Of course the two of them have already discussed this.

"She cut out after about ten minutes."

"Ouch." Noah winces.

I nod. "Went to the bathroom and never came back. Had our server slip me a note."

This time, all three of them wince.

"I think we need to give him some lessons. Dating 101," Noah says. "I didn't realize you were in such dire straits, Nicky."

"Dating 101?" I scoff. "I don't want dating advice from you guys."

"You clearly need it," Cash says, agreeing with Noah. "Piper and Angie won't have any friends left at the rate you're going through them."

"What do you think Dating 101 would look like for him?" Troy asks.

The three of them go off on a tangent that I can't help but laugh at.

Dating 101? If only they knew…

Whatever these three think they could drum up wouldn't hold a candle to lessons with Bex.

Thinking about her has a smile fighting to break out onto my face. I don't want to give these guys anything.

Right now, this thing with Bex is between the two of us. I have no idea how I would even begin to tell them that I'm dating her.

They'd probably think I was lying, if I'm being perfectly honest.

"Why don't you seem as upset as the last time?" Cash asks, breaking through my thoughts.

"Because I'm not," I state matter-of-factly. "It didn't go well. What's the point in getting upset about it? She said there was someone else."

"Okay, Angie is off the list for setting him up," Noah tells Troy. "I think I might know someone."

"Or none of you can find someone for me. You all clearly suck at this."

"Don't I get a try?" Noah asks, playfulness lacing his voice. "You would deny your best friend the chance to find you true love?"

I roll my eyes at that as Cash scoffs.

"What about Piper?" Cash asks. "They are besties too."

"Piper set him up with the influencer, remember?" Noah tells him. "It did not go well."

The whistle blows—thank God—starting practice again.

"I've got someone," Noah says before he skates away.

I laugh, shaking my head as the goalies coach skates over to work on drills. I love that the guys went all in with trying to set me up with someone, but how do I tell them I no longer need their help?

Sure, I have no idea where this thing with Bex will go —is it *just* hooking up? Or more?

I push all those thoughts out of my head as I practice my legwork. Getting knocked down and bouncing back up is key as a goalie. Even if my knees are going to be screaming at me by the end of the day.

It at least gets the guys off my back for a few hours. As Coach Barney dismisses us in waves, most of the guys are already gone by the time I'm done with practice. It lets me get cleaned up in silence.

No chirping from the guys about needing dating lessons. Or being set up with someone that they know.

Grabbing my bag, I head down the hall toward the players' parking lot to wait for Noah, who always takes more time cleaning up than most, when a sexy brunette catches my eye.

Bex is coming out of Coach Barney's office when our gazes lock.

"Hi."

"Hi," she says back.

Bex practically glides toward me, and it's hard not to watch her. The sway of her hips. The way her smile is lighting up her face. The happiness glowing in her eyes.

Fuck. Now that I've had her, all I want to do is stare at her. Let myself get lost in how gorgeous she is and the fact that this thing happened between us.

"Have a good night?" I ask, standing a few feet away from her.

"Mmm, a very good night." There's a sparkle now in her eyes. "Terrible date that somehow ended on a good note."

"A really good note, if I do say so myself."

"Very good." Bex nods to me.

I wish we weren't in the middle of the hallway. I want to pull this woman into my arms and ravish her mouth. Taste what I tasted last night. How fucking delicious she is.

"Hey Ms. Hart." Noah waves, coming out of the locker room. "Nicky, I'll text you that girl's number. Meet me outside if you still want a ride."

Noah doesn't glance back as he leaves the practice rink.

"Will do," I call after him, not looking his direction because I'm solely focused on the woman standing in front of me.

"A new date it sounds like?" Bex crosses her arms, eyeing me. "Are you planning on going?"

I take a step closer to her. There's still too much distance between us, but I can't do anything about it.

"See, they told me about this woman."

"Who is she?"

"I don't know."

"Why not?" Bex asks.

"I told them no."

"No?"

"Because I happen to like the woman I met at the bar last night a lot more."

Bex looks both ways before taking another step into me. This close, I can smell her perfume. It was all over me last night at home. I've never met someone who smells so fucking sweet that I want to keep that scent on me.

"Was she a nice woman?"

I waggle my head. "I don't know if you would call what we did last night *nice*."

"Far from it, it sounds."

"Something I'm hoping we get to do again?"

It's a question. Not exactly something we discussed last night in a rush to leave the bathroom so no one found us. That wouldn't have been a good ending to the night.

"Again and again, if you're up for it. Maybe work in a lesson or two?"

"Yes," I answer without hesitation.

"Then why don't you come over tonight, Nick?" Bex whispers. "See if we can find something *nicer* to do."

She couldn't stop me if she tried.

Chapter Thirteen

NICK

"You need to be on your best behavior, Oreo."

His black nose twitches. The small bundle of black-and-white fur looks up at me like I'm crazy. Which, I likely am because I'm telling my bunny to be on his best behavior. Not like he has any other kind of behavior.

He hops around in his play pen most of the day and eats and drinks whenever it's time to feed him.

The perfect companion for me and my crazy schedule. When I'm gone on road trips, my older neighbor who lives across the hall with her cat watches him.

And now I'm bringing him over to Bex's—my, well, I don't know what to call her. Girlfriend isn't appropriate. Partner doesn't fit either.

Friends with benefits kind of fits the bill, but I feel like it cheapens what we have. A quick screw every now and then? Not really what we have.

Not something I need to worry about as I step out of my car and take Oreo into my arms. Before I can even knock, Bex is there, pulling open the door.

"Hey Ni— You brought Oreo!" Her eyes immediately drop to Oreo's, whose nose is madly twitching away.

Using two gentle fingers, she strokes the fur between his eyes. Bex has the look on her face of anyone who comes into contact with something small and cute. Even though she's already met him once, she's still just as excited to see him again.

"I didn't want to leave him at home since I've been gone most of the day."

"Can I hold him?"

"Sure." I pass him over and Bex coos at him as she walks inside.

"I'm so happy you're feeling better, Oreo." Bex sits down on the couch and cuddles him in her lap. Oreo only sniffs at her, investigating Bex now that he's more like himself.

If you ask me, Bex sitting there with Oreo is about the cutest damn thing in the world.

"Noah wasn't home to watch him?" Bex looks up at me with happy eyes. Makeup still lines her face, even though she changed out of her work clothes from earlier into a pair of yoga pants and a Black Diamonds T-shirt.

I shrug a shoulder and drop down next to her. "He had other plans, and I figured you wouldn't mind having him over."

"I don't mind at all."

"I'm glad." I throw my arm around her on the back of the couch and pull her closer. The sweet, candy smell of her perfume infiltrates my every sense and scrambles my brain.

She nods, letting herself sink into my touch. "I'm also glad you didn't think to tell other dates about this, because I'm glad I have this all to myself."

"Mmm." I drag my nose along her jaw and nip at her ear. "You do."

She tilts her head, letting me kiss the exposed skin of her neck.

"All to myself," Bex moans. "Nick…"

Fuck. Listening to how turned on she gets makes me so damn hard, I'm punching a zipper pattern into my dick.

"Let me get Oreo set up so I can have my way with you."

Bex watches as I pull out a small, collapsible play pen for Oreo and set a few toys inside. Dropping a kiss to his soft fur, I put him in the pen and then turn my attention back to the woman consuming my thoughts.

"Upstairs."

I pull Bex up from the couch and motion her toward the stairs. She steps in front of me and leads the way. The oversized T-shirt she's wearing does nothing for her, but I know what lies beneath. I can't wait to get my hands on her.

Turning on the landing, I follow her toward her room. No words are said, but the tension is thick.

We both want this. I ache for this woman in every possible way. When I'm not with her, I'm thinking about her. I may be in too deep already, but fuck it. I'm past the point of caring.

Dropping down on the king-size bed that takes up the majority of Bex's room, it's the only thing I notice before I pull her onto my lap. Her fingers find purchase in my hair, twisting the strands to turn my gaze to hers.

As if it would be anywhere but on her.

"What do you want, Nick?"

I slip my hands up and under her shirt. Her skin is so warm and so damn soft, it makes it hard to breathe. I let my hands drift farther up, connecting with the soft fabric of her bra.

"I want to devour you, Bex. Savor every inch of your skin and make you so wild, that you'll be begging me to make you come."

"Mmm."

"I want to see you riding my cock. These beautiful breasts of yours"—I squeeze them for good measure and watch her face twist in pleasure—"bouncing as you come. Maybe even fucking them."

"Yes. God yes." Her voice is breathy, heavy with need.

I grab at the hem of her shirt, push the fabric up and over her head, then dump the T-shirt on the floor. Bex's chest is heaving with need. Clutching her in my arms, I flip us over and move her into the center of the bed.

Having her splayed out like this under me makes me want to do every dirty thing I've ever thought of to her. Settling between her legs, I trace one finger over the cups of her bra, watching as goose bumps break out over her skin.

"I picture this," Bex tells me.

"Picture what?"

I trace the strap of her bra up to her shoulder and tug it down. I repeat it on the other side.

"You. Doing this to me."

"When do you picture it?" I growl.

"When I have to get myself off."

Fuck. Me.

Leaning over her, I tug the cup of her bra between my teeth and release her breast. Her nipple is already diamond hard as I flick my tongue over it.

"Fuck, Bex. Show me what you do. Let me do it to you."

Bex squirms under me. "You're doing it. I love when you play with my nipples. They're so sensitive."

Kissing my way across her chest, I pull down the other cup and kiss my way around the tender skin there. Not quite giving her the attention where she really wants it.

"Nick," Bex moans. "Stop toying with me."

I give her nipple a quick peck before drawing up and staring down at her. Her lip is swollen from biting down on it, and her hair is already a mess.

We've barely gotten started, and I love seeing how worked up with need she gets. Grasping the thin material of her pants, I pull them off and toss them behind me. A wet spot is visible on the light color of her underwear.

Dragging my nose up her leg, I nip at her thigh. Every inch of skin on display, I lick and suck. Taste and savor.

I'm dizzy with lust as I rock back onto my knees between her spread legs.

"What do you want?" she breathes.

I look down at the erection tenting my pants. "Take it out."

Bex scrambles to her knees and undoes the button and zipper on my jeans with deft fingers. She wastes no time reaching into my boxers and pulling me out.

"Can I suck it?"

Watching this woman—this powerful, badass woman —taking command is the biggest turn-on. A heady feeling I want to ride for as long as I can. I can only nod at her before she pushes me onto my back. When she sucks the tip of my dick into her warm, wet mouth? I damn near lose my mind.

"Fuck!" I throw my head back as she laps at the precum. "You are so good at that."

I can feel her smile as she takes more of me in her mouth. I let her set the pace to start. Bex's hand wraps around the base of my cock as she pulls off me before sucking me back down. Fisting my hands in her hair, I slowly start to increase the pace. The way she peers up at me through hooded eyes has my dick thickening. The gagging and sucking sounds are the only thing I can hear as her expert tongue does things to drive me wild. My skin is on fire from how heated I am at her touch.

Bex's nails dig into my thighs as I slow her movements. "Fuck, Bex. I'm going to come."

She pops off me, wiping at her mouth. "Where do you want to do it?"

"Where? Fuck, I want to come on your breasts. In that sweet pussy of yours. In your mouth."

"Good thing the night is just beginning." Bex pushes up, clasping her hands behind my neck. "I'm going to ride you, just like you said. And once we've both recovered, you can come in my mouth. Deal?"

"Deal."

She seals it with the barest hint of a kiss. It has me chasing her mouth down, but before I can get what I want, she throws me down on the bed.

"Condom?"

I nod and she fishes my wallet out of my pocket. Ridding myself of my jeans and boxers, I rest my heads behind my head. Bex kisses the tip of my cock before ripping open the condom and rolling it over my hard length.

Her fingers drag along the other side in a teasing manner.

"What are you waiting for?" I bite out. I'm dying to get inside this woman. To feel her pussy choke my dick in the way only she can.

"Not so fun when you're teasing now, is it?" Bex cocks

a perfectly manicured brow at me before sliding her underwear to the side and sitting down on my cock.

She doesn't take her time. She doesn't move slow. Bex sinks all the way down to the hilt, and fuck me. It's perfect.

A bliss and heaven I've never felt before. At the restaurant, it was a frenzied combustion of nerves.

Now, Bex is taking her time. Almost like trying to prove a point by taking back control. If she wants it, she can have it.

Bex swivels her hips ever so gently, and it has me thrusting my hips up into her.

"You feel amazing, Nick. Like you were made for me."

"Mmm, yes." Grabbing her hips, I start to move her faster. "You're perfect, Bex. So fucking perfect, I can't stand it."

Smiling down at me, Bex rests her hands on my pecs and grinds down on me. I meet her every move with a thrust of my own. We're in perfect sync. Working in tandem to get each other off.

Bex is getting closer the more her moves become frazzled.

"Yes. C'mon, Bex." I move my hand to her clit and thrum it with two fingers. "I know you're going to come for me like the good girl that you are."

"Nick. Oh Nick!"

Bex comes on a quiet cry, throwing her head back. Her chest is bright pink as she rides me through the waves rolling over her.

My balls draw up tight, exploding as she takes me over the edge with her. "Fuck!" I grunt, grabbing a hold of her and keeping her locked down on top of me. "Fuck, fuck, fuck!"

I unload everything I have into the condom. My skin

feels too tight, like I'm going to burst out of it at how good I feel right this very instant.

The only person to ever make me feel like this is Bex. Sex has never been this good before. I don't know where this confidence has come from, but the woman now slumping over me brings it out.

Sweeping her hair back, I pull her face to mine. "Perfect, Bex. So. Fucking. Perfect. Bex."

I pepper each word with a kiss to her blissed-out face. Bex's eyes are pools of lust, and it has me wanting to puff out my chest because I did this to her. I brought this woman to her knees.

"Perfect," she murmurs, resting her head against my chest.

Neither one of us makes any move to get cleaned up or detach from one another. I could spend the rest of my life in Bex's arms and die a happy, happy man.

This may have started under the guise of us needing help at the whole dating thing, but it doesn't feel like that anymore.

Not now when there are feelings involved.

Feelings that keep growing every time I'm with this woman.

I only hope she feels the same way. Otherwise, I'm going to get my heart shredded.

Chapter Fourteen

NICK

"Alright men. Tonight is going to be a hard game," Coach Barney starts his pregame speech. "Carolina is a good team, and I don't want you underestimating them. We've been playing well on this road trip, and let's finish it off with a win."

He nods to Troy who brings all the guys into a huddle in the middle of the drab visitors' locker room. The black lockers are basic with one hook each for our suits. Not the most welcoming of locker rooms I've ever been in. Even our visitors' room is better than this.

Their way of trying to intimidate their opponents.

"Let's drown out all the noise tonight and work on playing the Black Diamonds hockey I know we can. We've worked hard this season, so let's keep it going. Black Diamonds on three. One, two, three…"

"Black Diamonds!" echoes around the locker room from all the guys.

Troy stands at the door of the locker room and gives each guy a fist bump as we head out onto the ice.

Boos echo around the arena as we're announced as the

visiting team. The guys start their own warm-ups while I head to the crease, scuffing it up to get ready for the game tonight before the pregame and anthems start.

Carolina's arena is one of the newer ones in the league. Lights flash around the different concourses in the team's colors. Music rocks through every inch of the place. A lone banner from a Stanley Cup win a few years ago hangs in the rafters above.

My eyes scan the crowd. It's a sea of gray and yellow with their team colors. Occasionally, I spot a Black Diamonds jersey thrown into the mix—the die-hard fans that will travel to the closest arena to watch us play.

I pause when I spot the box that I know Bex is in tonight. She's been with us on this trip.

I try not to let myself get too deep into my thoughts about her. Especially what we did last night. The last thing I need is to lose this game because I'm thinking about Bex riding me. Should I have snuck into her suite?

No. But damn if it didn't feel good to burn the excess energy I had from our win against Tampa.

My attention is brought back to the game as all the guys get in position for the puck drop. As soon as it hits the ice, it's all hockey.

It's the only thing that's important.

Carolina wins the puck and heads straight into our defensive zone. Cash is there, ready to defend as he scoops up the puck from an errant pass. Shooting it up to Troy, they move in sync.

Troy. Noah. Back to Troy. Over to Wright before he sends it sailing back to Troy, ready to shoot it at the goal. But Carolina's goalie is good and snatches it out of the air with his glove.

No easy goals.

Our guys are fluid, skating hard, working as one as they set up the play to try and get one into the net.

The puck is tipped off one of the guys' sticks, and Carolina is able to get the ricochet off the boards.

Carolina moves as one as they skate down the ice toward me. I'm ready. Cash moves into the defensive zone and prevents a breakaway. Another player for Carolina sends the puck to their center, who passes it off immediately.

The play is setting up, but our guys are there, fighting for the puck right in front of the net. There's a scrum and before I can process who has the puck, Carolina steals the puck from under the chaos and their winger is firing it right over my glove.

The horn sounds, the lamp lights up, and the crowd erupts.

"Fuck!" I slam my stick against the bar. It was an easy top-shelf goal that I let in.

"We'll get it back!" Cash shouts as he skates behind the goal. "It's only one goal."

I nod in his direction, grabbing my water bottle to take a swig. Like he said, it's only one goal.

As play resumes, my eyes are laser focused on the game. The guys are fighting hard in our offensive zone, but no luck putting the biscuit in the basket.

Damn. Carolina is good. You can only glean so much from watching film instead of live action. They picked up a few new players this season and they're gelling well.

But we're better. Even if the score doesn't show it as the horn sounds to end the first period.

"Don't get in your head, Nicky," Troy tells me as we head down the tunnel.

"It was an easy one."

"Nah, Cash was there and it snuck in. You'll get the next one."

Except, when the game resumes, it's another goal for Carolina to start the period. The crowd is going crazy with how fast they scored. Many seats are still empty, fans getting beers and food, and they missed the goal.

I ignore the chirping from the Carolina fans as the team celebrates on the ice.

Fuck.

I am not making the team look good tonight.

Thankfully, Noah is and gets one in the goal for us. He skates down the boards, fist-bumping everyone on the bench.

Good. 2-1 isn't the worst deficit to try and overcome. Not with plenty of hockey left to play.

The rest of the second period goes by without a goal. Both teams are equally matched tonight, and have been getting the shots on goal.

"That was a better second period, men," Coach Barney tells us once we're in the locker room for intermission. "Keep firing away, and we'll get there. Like I said, Carolina is a good team and we knew this would be a hard fight. Let's clean up those mistakes and play some good, hard hockey in the final period to bring this one home."

I take a few deep, steadying breaths to clear my head before we head out for the final period. It's never easy being down. It takes less than a second to score, but you can remain scoreless for an entire period before finally getting a scoring chance.

It won't be easy, but I'm ready to bring this game home for us.

The third period is a defensive battle, scoreless for the first half of the period. Carolina races down the ice, but

I'm ready. I knock the puck away with my stick, and Cash is there to take possession.

Troy is with him as he passes the puck off and is on a breakaway. It's him and the goalie. Pulling his stick back, he fires and it dings off the crossbar, hitting it out of bounds into the net that protect the crowds from wayward pucks.

"Damn it!"

It would've been a thing of beauty had it gone in. It's the way the rest of the period goes for us. Missed opportunities and good goaltending by Carolina.

No matter what we do, we can't seem to get the puck into the net. Carolina is matching us play for play.

With only two minutes left, Coach Barney calls me off the ice and sends in another guy to try and even up the score, but no such luck.

The final horn sounds in Carolina's favor.

Final score 2-1, Carolina.

They are going to be a good team for years to come, even if I hate to admit it. It's hard not to hang my head as I skate off the ice toward our locker room.

The mood in the locker room following a loss is never easy. Every single guy in here is carrying the blame solely on their shoulders.

I waste no time shucking off my pads and heading to the showers. The water is lukewarm at best as I'm in and out in a few minutes' time. The sooner we're all done, the sooner we head home.

The press is already waiting to talk to us.

What can you do to clean up your mistakes?

What did you think of that blocked shot that Hollins had in the third period?

Do you like your chances to make the playoffs?

Is it because there's a woman at the helm of the team?

I ANSWER every question with short, rote answers. This is one of the things I hate most about my job. Being in the spotlight.

All I want to do is play hockey. Everything else that goes with it? I'm not a fan. But I put on the best face I can in light of the loss and answer their questions. No matter how stupid they are. Especially that last one.

We'll study film tomorrow and work on what we can to ensure we have a better game next time.

It's the way of the game. Not every shot is going to go in, no matter how good you think they are.

It's still early, and the Black Diamonds are in a good position to make the post season again.

I HAVE to keep my cool because what else can I say? It's not Bexley's fault we lost. The better team won the game. It has nothing to do with the fact that a woman is our GM. Fucking asshole.

By the time I get settled onto the bus, we're only

waiting on a few more guys to finish up their interviews before we leave.

"That was a good game, Nick," Bex tells me as she passes by me. "Don't let them get in your head."

I nod in acknowledgment to her and peer over my shoulder as she heads to her customary seat at the back of the bus. She likes it there—less noisy, she once said, away from the guys.

I wish she could sit by me. Tell me that again to help push this loss out of my head. Damn. Bex is someone I'm quickly becoming addicted to.

I shouldn't be. Maybe if I keep telling myself that this thing will fizzle out, it'll help soften the blow. But when I peek back again, her eyes are on me, shooting me a wink.

I don't think this thing is going to fizzle out anytime soon.

Chapter Fifteen

NICK

I buckle my seatbelt as soon as I board the plane. All I want to do is get home, cuddle with Oreo, and sleep in my own bed. That's the hardest part of these long road trips. Being away from home.

"Don't take it too hard, Nicky." Coach Barney bumps me on the shoulder as he walks by on his way to his seat. "Carolina played hard tonight."

"I know."

Even if I hate it.

I'm in my own little bubble on the plane, taking up an entire row to myself. I don't want to have others give me platitudes about how I'll brush it off and win the next one.

Carolina was the better team tonight, plain and simple. It doesn't make the sting lessen.

The plane takes off and levels to cruising altitude.

The mood is depressing as fuck. After a win, the team is always ready to play cards or video games together, but now everyone's sitting and sulking in their own seats.

My eyes glaze over as I stare at the twinkling lights below us. I'm replaying every shot on goal that the opposing team had tonight. I know losses are never the result of one person, but as the goalie, it weighs on me.

I'm the final line between the other team getting the biscuit in the back of the net. I hate it.

"Mind if I sit?"

My gaze snaps to the person now standing at the end of my row.

Bexley.

"Sure."

I grab my headphones that are sitting in the middle seat and watch as she takes the empty seat on the aisle.

Even flying, Bex looks gorgeous, wearing a cowl-neck, deep-green sweater that clings to her curves and dark gray pants. Her dark hair is tossed up onto her head with black-framed glasses sitting on her nose.

"How are you taking the loss?" Bex asks quietly.

Glancing over the seats, all the overhead lights are off except one in the back. Coach Barney always sits and reviews the game on his own on our way home. The deep-purple glow of the lights over the bulkhead cast a soft light through the plane.

"Eh." I shrug a shoulder.

"It's not your fault."

"In the grand scheme of things, I know this. Hell, it's not even in the top ten of my worst losses."

"Oh really?" She quirks a brow at me, shifting in the seat to cross one leg over the other. I do my best not to focus on wanting them wrapped around me. "Alright then, what was your worst loss?"

"Are you really asking me that right now?" I shoot back, mirroring her pose and shifting closer to her.

"You got better things to do, Nick?"

The look on her face is one that would make me spill my deepest and darkest secrets to her. There's something about her that I trust. Maybe it's because this thing between the two of us is only between us, but even if it ended tomorrow, I know she wouldn't go airing my dirty laundry to the press.

"Alright, fine."

"Good. Tell me." Her dark eyes are focused on me, so intense. Always so emotional and telling me what she really feels.

This time? Victory.

"Well, I think my worst loss was in college. We got shut out and lost the game, seven to nothing. Two players had hat tricks, and it was one of the worst games I've ever played. It seemed like every time the puck came my way, it went into the back of the net."

"Seven to nothing? Wow, had I known that I might not have drafted you."

"Ouch." I laugh. "Glad to know what you really think of me."

"Stop it." Bex brushes me off, her hand ghosting over my forearm. It sends a frisson of energy racing through me. "You know you're one of the best goalies the Black Diamonds have ever seen."

On nights like tonight, I don't feel like it. I hate that I let our fans down. The team I have around me.

"Hey," Bex breaks into my own train of thought. "You know you're not the only person out there on the ice. It's a team effort. Every single one of those guys could have played better."

"I know, but—"

"No buts."

This time, when she drops her hand on my forearm, she leaves it there. Her thumb traces the protruding vein there. I watch, entranced by the slight touch she's giving me right now.

"I know you'll look at the film tomorrow and see what you can clean up before our next game, but that's it. That's all you can do," she tells me.

"You have a shockingly clear perspective on this."

"It was my dad's perspective during his playing days. You knew he played, right?"

"I knew he played, but didn't know how calm and collected he was. Apparently he passed on all his zen behavior to you."

Bex stifles a laugh with her hand, likely not wanting to draw any attention to us.

"Everything I know about the game, I learned from my dad. Surely your dad taught you how to handle losses."

"Whenever they lost, it never felt like it was the end of the world."

"That's because it's not," Bex says. "It might feel like that at the time, but losing a game isn't world ending."

I shake my head, trying not to drop my own hand down over Bex's. I relish her touch. The warmth that it sends through me.

"Pops was always good about that. Dad would come home, and whatever we were doing, he fit himself right into it. Coloring. Reading. Playing a made-up game. I think it helped everyone with the losses."

Bex pulls her hand away and I hate the loss. "My dad wasn't the best player, so he never seemed to take the losses as hard. He had the heart and the drive, but the talent was never there to back it up."

"He had a few good seasons with the team," I tell her.

"You would know, wouldn't you?" A sly smile creeps onto her face.

"I had to do my research on the owner of the team that was drafting me. I think he had more potential than he saw in himself."

Bex drops her elbow onto the armrest and rests her chin in her palm. "I think he saw a lot of himself in you."

"What, really?" That has me stopping and pausing.

"He saw the drive he had, but you also had the talent. He wanted to keep Denver's hometown kid here."

"Wow." I scrub a hand over the back of my neck. "I never knew he thought that."

I never knew Bex's dad played such a role in drafting me.

"He liked being involved."

"So why did he hand over the team to you?"

This isn't something the two of us have ever discussed. Sure, I know more about her in other ways, but not this. This seems like a pretty big oversight, and I'm kicking myself for not asking her before.

"He's getting older. Hockey has been his world for so long, that I think he needed a change."

"Not that my opinion means much, but I think you're doing great."

"It means more than you know, Nick."

God, I wish I could kiss her right now. With the soft light of the plane, she looks fucking gorgeous. I don't know how in the world she gave me a second look that night at the bar, but I'm so fucking thankful she did. I've been completely taken with her ever since.

"You know, sometimes it's still hard to believe that my dad handed over the team to me at all." She breaks through my perusal of her.

"Really? Why do you say that?"

"I'm the only female general manager in the league. I can't imagine a lot of people advised him to do that."

"Well, you know your shit," I tell her matter-of-factly. "In fact, I'd be hard-pressed to find someone who knows the game like you do."

Bex brushes off my praise. "Any one of the guys on this plane could do it."

"You're not giving yourself enough credit. I mean, I wouldn't trust all of these guys with a team. Noah? It's why I'm Oreo's main parent."

That earns me a warm laugh.

"Who better equipped to take over than you? You've grown up around this game, Bex. You're doing great."

"I wish I could believe that, but some days it's hard. Like tonight when Carolina's GM just brushed me off after the game. It sucks."

"Well, he's a dick, so I wouldn't worry about him."

Bex shakes her head. "I have to play nice with all of them. You never know when you'll need their help."

"Put him in his place. Maybe make him cry to bring him down a peg or two."

"You think I can?" There's a sparkle in Bex's eyes now.

"I've seen you bring grown men to their knees."

Her gaze is careful, calculated, as it brushes over me. "And by grown men, you mean you?"

"You can bring me to my knees anytime, Bex."

The plane dips as it hits turbulence. Instead of leveling out, it continues shaking. Great. Just what I wanted right now.

The intercom crackles to life. "It looks like we've hit a pocket of turbulence. We're going to try and find some smoother air, but until then, I'm turning on the seatbelt sign, and I want everyone to remain seated until we make our way through this."

A few groans echo around the cabin, likely because they were woken up.

Bex grimaces as she stands. "I should probably head back to my seat."

"Okay."

I don't want her to go, but I know she can't stay.

Text me she mouths to me.

I only nod as I watch her find her seat. I would do whatever she asks of me. Because that's how far gone I am for this woman.

The GM of my team.

A woman who is more than a decade older than I am.

All of that is background noise. Because it pales in comparison to how she makes me feel.

Which is, for the first time in my life, alive.

Chapter Sixteen

NICK

"Look who finally decided to show up." Dad's voice rings out over the couch as I close the front door to my childhood home.

"I don't make the schedule, Dad," I tell him, toeing off my shoes in the entryway.

The house is exactly the same as when we were kids. The walls might be a new shade of gray, photos changed out with ones of our growing family, and the sofa replaced with a newer, less flattened model, but it's the same cozy house I grew up in.

Walking into the living room that opens up to the kitchen, I see Pops is there watching over a pot of something that permeates the house.

It smells incredible.

"Thanks for finally making time for your dads," he calls out.

Dad pulls me in for a one-armed hug before unmuting the nightly sports broadcast.

"Again, I don't make the schedule."

"You barely called us while you were gone," Dad says. "It's like you've forgotten about us entirely."

"Always so dramatic." I laugh. "I texted you."

"Did you hear that, Carter?" Dad calls out. "He texted."

Pops comes into the living room with a glass of wine for Dad and a bottle of water for me. "Thanks."

"Next time, call," Pops admonishes. "We need to hear your voice to know you're doing okay."

"I'm twenty-three. I don't think you need to check on me anymore."

Dad claps me on the knee. "Nick, you're our son. We will always be checking on you. Even in your forties."

"So make sure you call, or we'll start popping by your place."

The last thing I want is for them to randomly drop by. Not that Bex and I are ever there, but if I'm not, that will raise questions. Questions I don't want to answer.

"What's that face for?" Dad asks, pushing his glasses farther up his face.

He's more gray than brown now, but other than that, he doesn't look like he's aged at all. I hope I have his good genes and age as gracefully as he has.

"What face? There was no face."

"Uh-uh, no way. You're hiding something."

"Am not," I fire back.

"Nick, that's exactly what you say when you are hiding something. Has Angie taught you nothing?" Pops comes back into the living room now.

"Who's hiding something?"

I groan, burying my face in my hands. Of course Angie and Troy choose this moment to show up.

"Your brother."

"What are you hiding?" Angie shrugs out of her coat and throws it over the back of the couch. "Do you know what he's hiding?" She turns on Troy.

He throws his hands up in defense. "Why are you asking me? I don't know what's going on. All I know is he took a hard hit in practice today."

"You did?" Both of my dads' eyes swing to mine.

"Are you okay?"

"Do you need ice? Ibuprofen?"

"Have you talked to the coach about this?"

They fire off their questions as I shoot an annoyed face to Troy. "Thanks a lot, man."

"Sorry," he whispers. He heads to the kitchen and grabs three beers, passing one to Angie and myself, before cracking his open.

"I'm fine." I take a refreshing sip while trying to reassure my dads. "Nothing I haven't taken before."

"But during practice?" Dad asks.

"Stop worrying."

"Okay, but if that's not what you're hiding, what aren't you telling us?" Angie asks.

Damn. She's like a dog with a bone and won't ever drop something. I both love and hate this trait about her. It was great when we were little and we were on the same side. Now? Not so much when I'm on the receiving end.

"There's nothing to tell."

Four sets of eyes are all staring at me. Judging me. Trying to decide whether I'm telling them the truth.

I'm not. But I *can't* tell them the truth. My dads would blow a gasket if they knew I was seeing Bex. Not that they wouldn't approve, but I have a feeling they would see it as me needing a maternal figure in my life and blame themselves.

It's never been an issue, but I can see them making it one to justify my actions.

I've never been worried about Bex being so much older than I am. I think because of the way I grew up, I matured faster. Pops always said I had an old soul. Maybe that's why we're so drawn to each other and why it's so hard for me to connect with people my own age.

A timer goes off, breaking the staredown. Thank God.

"Saved by the timer," Dad says. "C'mon. You can help set the table."

Even though I no longer live here, we all still chip in at dinner. It's why I'm glad Colorado drafted me. I love my dads and being able to spend my free time here.

By the time we're seated with Pops's latest recipe creation—a take on pasta and jambalaya—the conversation has once again turned back to me and my dating.

"Have you had any more luck on the dating front?" Angie asks, scooping a heaping portion of the pasta, sausage, and chicken concoction into her bowl.

"I plead the Fifth."

The very wrong thing to say because Angie's eyes light up with excitement. "So this is what you're hiding."

"Ang, I'm not hiding anything. The date you set me up on didn't go well."

"Edith said she was intimidated by you."

"She was?" Troy and I ask at the same time.

"Nick is the least intimidating person I know," Troy tells her. "If she didn't like him, there are easier ways to say that."

"Ouch. Thanks, man."

"Okay, fine. Not Edith. What about someone Piper knows?"

"Or maybe you guys give it a rest for now?" I ask instead. "Let me focus on hockey."

Troy waves my comment off. "We're ready for Arizona. Their first string goaltender is out. Should make it easier for us."

"Oh, the joys of sports talk at the table." Pops laughs. "And here I thought I'd get away from it when Alex retired."

We all laugh at that.

"Really, Pops?" I tell him. "You thought you'd get out of sports talk in this house?"

"You love it," Dad says, squeezing his shoulder.

"Yeah, yeah." He rolls his eyes. "At least I'm not the disappointment and played hockey instead of football."

Dad bursts out laughing at Pops's words. "If you could play either sport, I would be shocked. I love you, Carter, but you are not coordinated enough for that."

"Have you tried hockey?" Troy asks, passing the basket of bread around.

Pops shakes his head. "Never. The closest I got to the rink was taking Nicky to practice."

"You were a really good hockey dad, though," Dad tells him.

"I was, wasn't I?" Pops looks at him with nothing but tenderness in his eyes. It's the same way Angie looks at her husband.

Like that person is their entire world and they would do anything for them.

It's the same way I want to look at Bex. I want to invite her here. To have dinner with my family. I know her dad is gone—somewhere in Europe—and that it's just her. Being at dinner like this makes me think how easily she would fit in with my family.

Except, we can't, even though I want more. Need more. But right now, we're stuck in this forbidden limbo that I don't know how to get ourselves out of.

"You okay, Nicky?" Dad asks.

"I'll be right back. Need to hit the bathroom."

I excuse myself and head directly for the stairs. I head toward my old room instead of the bathroom. Flopping onto the bed, I try to quell the thoughts stirring through my head.

Practically everyone I know is disgustingly in love. My sister. My parents. Piper and Cash.

And what do I have? A relationship with the one person I shouldn't be with.

"You okay?" Pops sticks his head in the doorway.

"I'm—"

"Don't say you're fine. You're not," he interrupts, dropping down into the chair across from me. The room looks nothing like it did while I was growing up.

I didn't get into hockey until I was in high school and hit my growth spurt. My room was always filled with books. I loved learning. Still do. But since I realized I could make a better career out of being a goaltender, I followed the money.

Besides, I can always go back to school when I'm done.

"Sorry. It's just frustrating."

"What's frustrating?" Pops leans forward, resting his elbows on his knees.

"Being around so many people in love."

"Why is it bothering you now?"

"I just wish I could find someone to bring home."

Not exactly a lie. Because I do want to bring Bex here more than anything.

"Is that code for you don't want to tell your old man?" He laughs. "Or you can't because you don't want me to know who you're dating, if you are dating someone, that is? You know you can tell us about whoever you're dating…man or woman."

"I know."

That's the one thing I never had to worry about. Growing up with two dads, I always knew it would be safe to love whoever I wanted to.

Except...what am I supposed to tell him? I'm dating the owner of the team? Someone who is more than a decade older than I am?

Not that I would call what we're doing dating. We haven't even given it a name.

"You'd tell us if something were wrong?"

"Yes, Pops. Nothing is wrong."

"You're just moping around like a teenager then for the fun of it?" I hear the laugh in his voice, and it helps break me out of my errant thoughts.

"Yes. I didn't get to do nearly enough of it as a teenager. Why not now?"

"Maybe because you're an NHL goalie and have a lot going for you?"

"I guess so."

"Five more mopey minutes, then downstairs for dessert. I got the pie you like from the bakery on Colfax."

"Thanks, Pops."

It's the one treat I allow myself during the season. Who doesn't love chocolate mousse pie?

I make good use of every one of the five minutes. It's what they let me do growing up. Any time things got bad at school or I was too in my head, they wouldn't let me wallow for more than five minutes. After that, they'd cheer me up by taking me to get a treat or a new book.

If I wasn't at the rink, I had my nose buried in a book. Maybe I need a book to figure out what the hell is going on with Bex.

Because the more I stew over her, the more I want her. And the more I realize I can't have her.

I wish I could stay up in my room and not be an adult. Things were so much easier as a kid.

Now, what the hell am I going to do about falling in love with the wrong person?

Chapter Seventeen

BEXLEY

"Hey."

Nick slides into my office, peeking behind him before he closes the door.

"Hi."

A grin appears on his face as he walks over to the desk and leans over to press a kiss to my lips.

"I've missed you," Nick says, leaning against the side of my desk.

"I have missed you too."

With so many meetings this week, I didn't go with the team to their game in Chicago. One away game and a quick there and back, I felt my time was better spent here. The director of operations had it down.

Even if I had to fight off more questions from the press about my qualifications to run the team.

Apparently playing hockey and a dick are the only two that are needed.

"I'm glad we have a few home games."

"Don't like traveling?" I fist my hand in his shirt and pull him down to me.

"Not without you."

Nick steals a kiss and I lean into him. My toes curl in my heels as he slides his tongue into my mouth. It's short and fast and damn it, I want more.

"You're mean."

Nick smiles against my mouth, tipping my face up to look at him. "Am I? Do I need to make you feel better?"

I mock a pout, nodding my head.

"And how would I make you feel better?"

Dropping his hands on either side of the chair, Nick hovers over me. From here, the blue of his team shirt stretches across his muscled chest. The one that I love tracing after we have sex.

It has my brain stirring and my lady parts waking up. It's been a few days since I've been with Nick. When we started this thing, I had no idea it would lead to this. Now that it has, I'm greedy. I want everything he will give.

Sex. Orgasms. Smiles.

"I need an orgasm." The words come unbidden.

"Is that so? Has your tutoree not been giving you what you need?"

I groan. "Not at all."

"I think I can take care of that for you."

Grabbing my hand, Nick pulls me up to stand, and I crash into his hard chest as his mouth slants over mine.

Heat and tension swirl around us as we both fight to take control of this kiss. Nick's hand in my hair tips my head back as he licks his way along my jaw.

"I want to fuck you, Bex."

I hold tight to him because I want it. More than I've ever wanted anything in my entire life.

"Do it, Nick."

Stepping back from him, I lean against the edge of my desk and start to undo the buttons on my blouse. The gray sweats Nick is wearing do nothing to hide his growing erection.

It's a mouthwatering sight to see how hard I make him.

"Are you wet for me, Bex?"

"Why don't you see?" I try to spread my thighs, but my skirt constrains them.

The smile Nick wears is downright devious as he pulls me to the edge of the desk, leaning me back so I don't topple over. Shoving my skirt up, Nick drags a knuckle over the wet spot on my cotton underwear.

"Are you always like this for me?" Nick kneels down, licking and sucking his way up my thigh. "Always thinking of me on my knees for you? Worshipping you like you deserve to be?"

Nick closes his lips over my clit, sucking it through my underwear, and I buck up into his mouth.

"Gah!" I cover my mouth with my hand, trying to be quiet.

Nick stops what he's doing, turning a wet smile to me. "You can't be loud. No one can know I'm in here."

I nod, keeping my hand where it is.

"Good girl. Now, if you're not, I'm going to have to punish you later."

"Maybe I want you to punish me."

He bites into my thigh, licking the sting away. "Noted, Bex."

It almost makes me want to be loud just so I can take what he dishes out. It's always the quiet ones. When we started this thing, Nick bumbled his way through every lesson. It was sweet, how nervous he got. But the second things escalated, it's like a switch flipped.

Gone was the Nick who was always nervous. In his place was a commanding man, who takes what he wants.

Who is kind and caring, but knows exactly what he's doing in the bedroom.

Where has this confident man been hiding, and how did I ever think he needed lessons?

The way he kisses is like he is memorizing every nip and dip of my mouth. The way his hands know exactly how to please me is like he's been doing this for years.

Nick Brooks-Young is a master of pleasure.

Pushing my underwear to the side, Nick blows warm air over my aching pussy. I drop my head back as his tongue slips inside me.

Between that and his fingers on my clit, I'm in heaven. Pure ecstasy as I let Nick work me over.

"Nick, I am so close."

I hear the soft rustle of fabric and look down to see Nick starting to jack himself off. The way his veined hand moves up and down his hard length has me squeezing down on his fingers.

"You like this?" he whispers against me. "Don't you know, Bex?"

"Know what?" I sink my fingers in his hair and pull his gaze up to mine.

"Know what you do to me? Fuck, you drive me crazier than any woman ever has."

"I feel the same way. I need you to make me come."

"Fuck, yes."

Nick turns his attention back to my dripping pussy. My brain is a wash of emotions, clogging my thoughts from anything other than this beautiful man's mouth on me.

But something else registers. Right before Nick pulls me over the edge, a knock sounds.

The fog in my brain resides as I take in the fear in Nick's eyes.

"Shit!" I gasp, popping up off my desk. "Umm, hide!"

"Where?" he hisses.

I can't imagine how I look right now. Skirt hiked up to my waist, blouse undone. Hair a mess and cheeks pink.

Nothing to kill a mood like someone about to come into your office.

"Under here."

I shove Nick under my desk, trying to fan my cheeks. I'm sure they are pink because, fuck me, I was so close to coming.

"Stay quiet and don't move," I hiss, hurriedly buttoning up my shirt. "Come in."

My voice sounds normal to my ears, or maybe that's wishful thinking.

The chair I'm sitting in moves ever so slightly and it's then I feel Nick's warm mouth on my inner thigh.

What in the hell is he doing?

"Sorry to bother you during lunch, Bex," Anna starts, "but a few notices came out from the league that need your review."

Anna stands in front of my desk, passing them over as Nick's lips move farther north, pushing my skirt up.

"Mm-hmm."

It's all I can manage when I feel a finger slide inside of me as I take the stack of papers.

"You have a meeting with Cassie on the books for two to discuss the All-Star weekend and what players were selected and then your weekly meeting with the press at three."

"Press. Meeting. Got it."

I'm repeating what she says, all common sense having fled my brain. Instead of hiding like I told him, Nick is whipping my emotions back into a frenzy.

"Are you okay?"

"Fine," I gasp out as Nick bites on my thigh again. Oh God.

This man is driving me absolutely insane right now.

"You sure?"

Steeling myself to sound normal, I squeeze my thighs around Nick's head and hope he gets the message.

"Yes. I have a few calls to make so see to it that no one disturbs me for the next hour or so."

Anna nods. "I'll let you know when Cassie gets here."

"Thank you."

I watch her as she leaves and listen for the door to click shut.

"What are you doing?"

I push back from my desk and there's a mischievous look in Nick's eyes.

"I told you…"

"When Anna was here?"

"What can I say?" He shrugs a shoulder and pops out from under the desk. "I wasn't going to let anything stop me."

"And now?" Now that Anna has left, all I want is for Nick to make good on his word and fuck me. "What are you going to do?"

Nick unfurls himself from below the desk, towering over me. "Bend over."

I waste no time, standing and leaning over my desk. The sound of a condom wrapper opening has me squeezing my legs together.

Nick's broad chest covers my back as he leans over me. "Are you ready for me?" He drags his cock through my wet folds. "Ready to feel me fill you up?"

"Yes. Don't make me wait."

Lining himself up, Nick slowly pushes inside. Not going all the way in, he holds himself steady.

"You bastard," I groan, squeezing the desk. "What are you waiting for?"

"I think I need to punish you now."

"For what?" I look over my shoulder to ask him. His lips are right there.

"For making me wait. Taking a meeting when I was going to make you come."

"Ugh."

I try to shift farther back onto his hard dick, but he doesn't let me move.

"Uh-uh. You want my cock?"

"You know I do." It's practically a whine. Having been so close only minutes before, I'm ready to snap. A live wire ready to explode.

"Then what will you do next time?"

"Next time?"

Nick nods against me, kissing and sucking on the tender skin of my neck.

"Wh-what do you mean, next time?"

I feel the smile as he brushes my hair to the side. "You don't think this is the only time I plan on doing this in here, do you?"

"We were almost caught!"

"Tell me you didn't like it."

"I didn't…"

He nips at my neck and pushes in another inch.

Damn him.

"No lying, Bex. Tell the truth."

"Fine. I loved it. I want you to fuck me in my office. Maybe next time up against the windows."

This gets me another two inches.

"Against the windows, you say? I think you have a bit of an exhibitionist streak in you."

"Any time I can have you, I want you, Nick."

On those words, he slams inside of me. Filling me. Stretching me.

"Yes!" I whisper-shout. "So good, Nick. So good."

"God, Bexley. Do you know how good you feel? So tight. So warm. So fucking perfect."

Nick sets an easy pace, pumping his hips in and out of me. The weight of his body over me is delicious. Every single one of my senses is on fire.

I was so close before, but now I'm right there at the edge. Taking everything Nick is giving me to finally get me over the top.

"The way you choke my cock." Nick's nose drags up my neck. "Nothing has ever felt better."

His hips move faster. I shift my head and bury my face in my arms so when I do come, it will be muffled.

"Are you there? Fucking come on me, Bex. Do it."

Nick jacks his hips once, twice, and then I'm exploding around him. My vision blurs in front of me as I ride the tidal wave flowing through me. It's a high I've never felt before.

Maybe it's because I've never done it in my office, or because we were almost caught. But something about this moment with Nick is better than every single orgasm I've ever had in my life.

And when he pulls back to move fast, I feel him come inside me. His words are garbled as he falls apart like I did.

"Holy shit," he pants out, collapsing on top of me.

The only sound in my office is our breaths. It smells like sex.

I can't remember the last time I've been fucked so good. All at the hands of a man who I was supposed to be teaching how to date.

Instead, he's teaching me how I should be treated. How a man *should* treat a woman.

I feel the loss of him as soon as he slips out. He pulls me up and we clean ourselves as best we can, then Nick plops down on my chair and I settle into his lap. We don't have much time before I have my next meeting, but I want to enjoy every second I can with him.

His strong arms wrap around me, fingers dragging up and down my sides. The tender way he is touching me makes my heart swell.

Almost like he's cherishing me. Almost like…he loves me?

I don't want to think about that. Because those feelings are too big for me to worry about right now. Not when I'm still under the hazy post-sex glow.

"You know, I think I've learned a lesson for next time."

"Oh yeah?" Nick presses a kiss to my temple. "What's that?"

"Next time, you lock the door."

His warm, rich laughter echoes out, filling me up inside.

"A lesson learned indeed."

Chapter Eighteen

BEXLEY

I wish I'd never started these.

Another week, another press conference.

It's the thought that goes through my head as I answer another one of the questions lobbed in my direction. Sure, Dad told me I didn't need to do these.

The need to prove myself to everyone though? I thought it would be a way to get in good standing with the fans.

A woman can only be asked so many times how the recovery of their star player is going without losing her mind.

Same as last week. And the week before that. And the week before that as well. The press doesn't want to hear that. They want an underlying reason, something juicy, as to why Noah Fields isn't recovering the way we'd hoped.

I guess it's better than them questioning my abilities to run the team. *I'll take what I can get.*

"Yes, Trent." I point to the familiar face in the front row. When I first met him, he had salted-brown hair. Now, it's completely white. I wonder if it's the stress of this job.

Even still, he's one of the few people in here I don't mind dealing with. Always fair and never spreading false rumors. The same can't be said for a lot of people here.

"Care to comment on the latest story with Sports Refresh?" he asks.

"Story? I'm not sure what you're referring to." This is the first time I'm hearing of this. Based on the gleeful look that washes over his face, he knows it too. Shit. Wasn't I just singing his praises and now he looks like the cat that got the canary.

"Their CEO has been asked to step down in light of using company money for extracurricular activities. Ones that are not family friendly."

Oh for fuck's sake. Of all things to land on my desk today of all days.

Sports Refresh is one of our biggest sponsors. Their logo is plastered all over the boards at the arena. Hell, I'm pretty sure their logos are all over the water bottles sitting in the locker room now. It might even be on the backdrop behind me. And this supposed "family-run company" has a cheating philanderer at the helm?

My day just got infinitely worse.

I straighten in my seat, my mask of indifference that I've learned over the years sliding into place. "As it is still a developing story, Trent, I will not comment until the full facts have been released. Thank you all for being here, but I have a meeting with our coach that I need to attend. Have a nice day."

Grabbing my tablet, my eyes dart to the backdrop. I hate being right sometimes. The logo for our biggest sponsor is right there, mocking me.

These are the days I hate my job. As soon as I find out who kept this from me, they are going to hate their job too.

I do my best to walk out of the room at an easy pace,

when all I really want to do is run down to my communications director and ask what the fuck is going on.

Throwing open the door, I see it's one less thing to do because Cassie is already waiting there for me.

"Bexley, I can explain."

"My office, now," I grit out, stalking in that direction. "Not here."

I don't want any prying eyes or recording mics to hear this conversation. There has to be a reasonable explanation as to why I didn't find out about this.

I make it a point to know everything that's going on that could affect my team. Trades among other teams, coaching changes. Hell, even a change in equipment managers I like to know about.

Anything that will give me an edge on my opponent to do better in my job, I take it.

To be blindsided like this has me fuming.

A flurry of activity is bustling as I push open the glass doors to the C-suite.

"Anna, please hold all my calls and cancel the rest of my meetings for the afternoon. No one in or out."

"Got it."

Her eyes trail behind me to Cassie and get even wider.

As soon as the door is closed, I turn to face my communications director.

"How in the world did this get by me? A sponsor of this size with a scandal like this? Why did no one make me aware of this?"

Shrugging out of my suit jacket, I throw it onto the couch behind me and take a seat. I tap into my tablet to see what I can find out about this scandal that is now affecting us.

Cassie shifts in front of me. "They were in damage

control mode. We were hoping that they would come out on the other end of it, but it doesn't appear that way."

I blow out a hard breath. "So instead of telling me about it, you let me get blindsided during my morning press conference."

"Not ideal."

"Not ideal is toast instead of an English muffin. A major sponsor that we will likely have to cut is a problem. We get millions from them every year, and now where do you think we're going to go?"

"What can I do to help? Do you want me to put out feelers for other sports drinks companies that are looking to expand?"

"I want a list of everyone that is interested in doing business with us by the end of the day. I don't care who it is. All should be vetted before they hit my desk to ensure they are squeaky clean."

"Yes. My staff is already on it. I'm working with marketing to ensure we have a reputable company going forward."

"Good. Is that all for today? Or am I going to find out that one of my players was arrested for indecent exposure?"

Cassie winces. "Nothing like that today. I'm so sorry, Bexley."

I shake my head. "Next time, tell me about this so I can be on the offensive."

"You got it, boss."

"Good. Now I need to get back to answering all these calls that are stacking up."

Cassie rushes out of my office with her tail between her legs.

I go back to my tablet and read all about the supposed

family man CEO of our biggest sponsor and his affinity for women who aren't his wife.

It's disgusting seeing all these women come forward. Some he worked with, some of them he met at a bar. The company released a statement, but it does little to combat all the bad press they've already gotten.

Just when I thought things were settling down.

Running this team isn't the easiest job in the world, but I love it. Hockey is in my blood, from the time I was born until I took an internship right out of college.

Even though my family owns the team, my dad wouldn't give me a job just because of the Hart family name. *You have to earn your success, Bex,* he always told me. *How would you learn otherwise?*

I've spent every minute here learning everything I can about the team and the league. I became a student of the sport and business. So when the time finally came for a position in the corporate suite, I was ready, until our GM retired and I got another promotion.

No two days are alike. A problematic player one day followed by a sponsor scandal the next.

Fuck. I need a glass of wine. If only it were appropriate to drink at noon on a Tuesday. Instead, I seek out the one person that I know will help.

BEX

I hope your day is going better than mine

NICK

Practice as usual. Getting ready to nap before the game tonight. How's everything up in the C-suite?

> Oh, just a major sponsor screwing anything with two legs and me getting blindsided by a reporter with that info. Just an average day

> Shit, Bex. Anything I can do to help?

THIS IS why I knew reaching out to Nick would calm the anger boiling inside me.

> Talking to you helps

> Well in that case, Oreo says he misses you

A PICTURE COMES through of the small bundle of fur resting on Nick's bare chest. I don't think I've seen anything cuter in my life.

> Aww…I miss Oreo too <<bunny emoji>>

> If only you could come over now…

IT'S ALL I WANT. To put the office in my rearview mirror and leave this bad day behind me. To curl up with Nick and have him to listen to all my worries about what is going on. It's a hard balancing act—to not unload too much of the team's inner workings onto him.

But eyeing my calendar, I know the All-Star break is coming up. With only Troy and Cash slated to play for our team, I make a split-second decision.

> Go away with me over the break

What? We can't. People would see us

> Not where I have in mind

I'm trying to think of a reason not to, but I can't

> Then say yes. I'm serious. I need to get away and not think about hockey

Yes

> For real?

I CLUTCH my phone to my chest, watching the three bubbles pop up then disappear. *Please don't take it back. Please don't take your yes back.*

I want this weekend with Nick now more than ever. It was a fleeting thought, but getting to take him to my favorite place in the world? I want to show Nick this side of me. To show him where I came from. A part of me that I never share with anyone.

Let's do it. You and me. That's all I need. Well, and maybe Oreo

I SMILE down at my phone, a picture of Oreo's face filling the entire screen.

> Oreo can come too

Nah, Noah will be sad without him.
Besides, I want to spend all my free time
with you

> You sure know how to make a girl feel
> special

I will spend the entire weekend doing
just that

> I can't wait <3

Chapter Nineteen

NICK

"Look who finally decided to come to guys' night!" Noah chirps.

"You realize this is the first one we've had in months, right?" I tell him, dropping the four large pizzas on the counter in our condo. None of us can ever decide on what we want, so it's always a pizza each.

Snacks—pretzels, chips, dips, and veggies to round out the night—already sit out in big bowls.

"Because you've been so busy."

"I have not," I tell him.

Noah drops onto the barstool across from me and pins me with a studying face. I don't back down from it. I know he's trying to glean whatever information he can out of me, but he won't get it.

No one—and I mean no one—can find out about me and Bex. I have no clue how the guys would react if they found out.

Hurt? Angry? Deceived?

It's not like I want to lie to them, but I can't tell them

the truth. One accidental slipup to the press, and it could blow up our relationship.

"Fine. I'm going to go feed Oreo." The buzzer sounds from the front of the condo. "You let them in."

"Got it."

Noah grabs two carrots from the veggie tray and stalks off to where Oreo's burrow is.

Buzzing the guys up, I wait with the door open as the elevator beeps at the far end of the hallway.

We're in one of the newer buildings of Denver. It's nice because everything still has that new-building shine. Even the smell feels like it's a new house when you walk inside.

It's not the biggest of condos. Noah and I each have our own space on either side of the living room and kitchen, with a small nook off the main room for Oreo. We're lucky we had space for a dining room table when we got this place.

Sure, the two of us could each have afforded our own place, but being this close to the rink and having someone to split the mortgage with isn't a bad thing. It's not like either of us are bringing a lot of dates home.

"Glad to see you cleaned up for us," Troy says, looking around our condo as he walks through the open door.

It's immaculate—as it always is. Considering how often we're at the rink for practice, or traveling for away games, we don't spend that much time here during the season.

The hardest part is cleaning up after Oreo. Who knew that the messiest thing in our apartment would weigh all of six pounds?

"Please. It's only clean because Nick lives here. If it were only Noah, you wouldn't see the floor," Cash tells me, walking by me to put a six-pack in the fridge.

"I take offense to that," Noah chimes in, coming back into the kitchen. "I'm not *that* messy."

I snort at that. I keep the communal space clean. Noah's room? A completely different story.

"Noah, we've all seen your locker. It's okay." Troy grabs a carrot and bites into it with a loud snap, chomping through a smile at Noah.

"I'm rethinking this guys' night now," he grumbles.

"You just don't want to lose all your money." I laugh. Opening a box of pizza, I grab a slice of pepperoni and banana peppers and slap it onto my plate before heading to the dining room table.

"Oooh, little Nicky with the trash talk," Troy chirps, ruffling my hair.

"Get off!" I try to shove him off me, but he wraps an arm around my shoulders and gives me a noogie. Like an annoying older brother would.

"Help!" I cry out, but I'm only met with the laughter of the other guys. Ducking out of his hold, I shove Troy away. "Now I'm really going to take your money."

"I've gotten good." Troy takes the beer Cash holds out to him, and I grab the other from him, nodding in thanks. "Carter has taught me a thing or two."

It's one of the ways Troy bonded with my pops—trying to get an edge on us during poker nights. I'll never tell him just how bad he really is. He loves getting to hang out with my dads like that, especially since his family still lives in San Diego.

"So you like to think," Cash states.

"Is this gang up on Troy night?" he huffs out. "I'm not liking this."

"You make it easy," Noah tells him, taking the seat next to me and grabbing his own slice of pizza from the second box—meat lovers.

"I'm losing my edge on you guys."

"What edge?" Cash asks. "You've never had an edge on me."

"Maybe I'm just letting you think I don't when in reality, I do."

"Wait, now you're confusing me," I tell them. "Who has the edge?"

"Troy, apparently," Cash says. "Or me? Hell, I don't know."

"It's a good thing we're better hockey players than insulters." Noah laughs, handing out plates to the guys to grab their dinner. "We'd all be epic failures otherwise."

"Insulters? Really?" Cash looks at Noah with a weary grin.

"What? I went to school with my mom the other day and one of the kids said the other kid was mean because he was an insulter, i.e., you guys."

There's a moment before all three of us break out into laughter. "Oh man, little kids. I can't wait to have some of my own," Troy says. "I hope none of them are insulters."

"Kids say the damndest things," Cash agrees.

"If you guys are ready, let's get this game started," Noah cuts in. "I'm ready to win some money."

"If you say so." Troy jabs his elbow into his side as he passes by him on the way to the table.

The felt poker table cover we use is already spread out. Poker chips sit in the middle, and an ice bucket filled with our favorite drinks is waiting for us.

Darkness has already settled outside, our reflections casting back at us in the windows. Each of us settles into our usual seats, grabbing various chips to start playing with.

Cash, having won the last game, starts dealing.

"Alright little Nicky. I think we've gone long enough.

How is dating going?" Cash asks as he starts dealing the cards.

"Yeah, you've been quiet on the whole 'set me up' thing," Troy agrees. "Even Angie says you're mum on the subject."

"That's because Angie is nosey," I tell Troy. "If I tell her anything, she'll tell you and our dads, who in turn will tell everyone they know. And I don't need that kind of pressure."

Noah's eyes light up with excitement as he takes his cards. "Does that mean there is someone?"

"I don't know if you're excited for me or for what you have in your hand." I stare him down, trying to get a reaction out of him.

Noah pulls his cards closer to his chest. "You'll just have to wait and find out."

I arrange my own hand, figuring out what to go for.

"You all knew when I was dating someone," Cash points out. "You have to tell us."

"There isn't anyone."

The lie tastes bitter leaving my lips. Could I trust these guys with the truth? Yes, but I don't want to worry about them letting it slip.

Bex isn't someone I want to hide. She's starting to mean everything to me. I want to shout it from the rooftops that we're together. But I don't want that kind of attention on us.

It'd rain down on us from all sides if we were found out.

"Raise." Troy breaks through my thoughts.

"Call." Noah flips his cards over and I do the same, my flush beating all of their hands.

"Damn it! How are you so good?" Troy gripes at me as I pull the small stack of chips to me.

"Lucky." I shoot him a playful grin as he shuffles the cards.

As the game goes on, the stack of chips sitting in front of me continues to grow, earning me annoyed glares from the guys.

Pulling in another stack of chips, I turn their angry glares into something I know they'll like talking about. "Are you guys excited about the All-Star game next week?"

"No," Noah grumbles. "Just means more PT for me to try and get back onto the first line."

"You'll get there." Troy tries to lift his spirits, but it's been hard on him. "Cash and I will make sure the team looks good."

"You bummed you didn't get picked, Nick?" Cash asks, dealing out another set of cards.

"No. I could use the break."

More so, I want the break that Bex and I have in mind. A weekend away at her cabin? It's all I can hope for.

I'm muttering to myself, playing the hand I'm dealt as Cash eyes me. "Hang on, are you counting the cards?" His jaw drops.

"Fuck you!" I balk at the insinuation, flicking a poker chip in his direction. "Just because I'm good and kicking your ass doesn't mean I'm cheating."

"I'm keeping that," Cash tells me, flipping me off.

"Wouldn't you know by now if I could count cards? Besides, you won last time." I point out to him.

"Maybe you let him win," Noah counters.

"You are just exceptionally bad, Cash," Troy agrees. "Sorry you're losing your money."

"Pretty sure Oreo is better than you, and he doesn't have thumbs," Noah confirms. "I never knew you liked losing this much."

Cash throws his cards down and grabs his empty beer bottle. "Screw you guys. I'm out this next round."

"Aww. Poor Willy. Can't take the heat," Noah chirps.

"More like a sore loser." I laugh.

It feels good being with the guys like this. We travel all the time, and live and room together on the road, but somehow it's different. There's not the pressure of a game to disturb our focus. It's a rare night off, and instead of them spending it with their loved ones, we're all hanging out together.

This is one of the things I love most about being on the team.

"If you do want us to try setting you up again, we'll make sure to thoroughly vet this person. Not like the last two."

I roll my eyes at Cash. Can't catch a break, I guess. "They were nice, but just not for me."

"Are you sure it's not a *you* problem?" Noah directs at me.

Before, I would've said yes. Turns out, all I needed was to find the right person. That person being Bex.

"I'll let you know when I'm ready."

Hopefully, I'll never need to take them up on it again.

Not if I have anything to say about it.

Chapter Twenty

BEXLEY

The biting sting of the air hits me in the face as I step out of the car. The clean mountain air is refreshing as I spin and take in the small A-frame cabin. Snow covers the green roof.

We're in the middle of nowhere. It's one of my favorite parts of coming out here.

No press. Not putting on a show for anyone. No incessant answering of questions that I continuously have to answer. Just me and the place that soothes my soul.

And Nick. I'm grateful that he came here with me. I want to show him the place that means so much to me because *he* means so much to me.

"This is where you spend your free time?" Nick asks, coming around to meet me, slipping into his coat as I zip mine up.

"It doesn't look like much from the front." Linking hands with him, I pull him toward the stairs of the front porch. Snow is piled on both sides, but there's a small walkway shoveled out for us by the caretaker of the place when I'm not here.

Punching in the code to the door and swinging it open, it smells like home. A mix of pine and fresh air that always clears every thought in my head as soon as I step foot inside.

Natural wood lines the interior. Being a smaller house, it's an open floor plan. A full-size kitchen with black marble counters is on the left with a cozy living room on the right. Photos of Dad and me with Mom line the wall above the stone fireplace. A set of stairs behind the kitchen lead up to the only bedroom that looks down over the living room.

Off a narrow hallway is the only bathroom and the back porch with the most incredible views of the forest beyond.

"It belonged to my mom," I tell Nick as he sets our bags down next to the pile of wood at the door. "After she died, my dad didn't want to change anything."

"I think it's perfect."

It warms my heart to hear him say that. I've never brought anyone out here before. This place is sacred to me. To my family. It feels right to have Nick here to share it.

"C'mon. Let me show you my favorite part." I drag Nick down the long hallway and push open the back door.

"Wow." His bright-blue eyes take in the deck that opens to a large, frozen pond. A hot tub takes up one side, and an empty firepit sits at the end of the stairs. "I can see why you like coming here."

Resting my elbows on the railing, I gaze out at the undisturbed land spread before me. "It's the one place that doesn't ask anything of me. Where I can be myself."

Warmth engulfs me as Nick comes up behind me. I let out a breath I didn't realize I was holding. "You know I don't ever expect anything of you, right?"

Spinning in his arms, I look up at the man casting a

long shadow over me. His nose is tipped red from the cold, and his eyes are attentively gazing at me.

It has my breath catching in my chest—the intensity with which he's looking at me. I shouldn't be feeling this.

Whatever *this* is.

He's *my* player.

But it's hard to stop the feelings from growing and blooming in my chest.

To the outside world, Nick Brooks-Young is the stoic goalie of the Colorado Black Diamonds. A force to be reckoned with in the crease. Never one to back down from a challenge.

To me?

He's one of the only people to see me for me. Not as the GM for the Black Diamonds. Not as a woman in a position of power.

"I know."

It's all I can say. Because everything else feels too big.

His warm hand cups my cheek before he dips down and presses a kiss to my lips. One that has butterflies erupting in my chest and my body leaning into his.

It's a gentle kiss, a promise of things to come.

Because Nick and I have the entire weekend together.

"Is it bad I'm glad you didn't go to the All-Star game?" I whisper against his lips.

"No. Because I'm glad too."

"Yeah?" I look up at him. A light snow has started to fall.

He nods, brushing his nose alongside mine. "I want to be here with you. My body needs the break."

"I hope not too much of a break."

A sly smile spreads across his full lips. "Not that much of a break, Bex."

"You have such a dirty mind." I laugh, reaching over to the railing to grab a fistful of snow and throw it at Nick.

"That was evil!" Nick shouts, trying to shake the snow out of his jacket.

I dodge out of his hold and bolt down the stairs. The snow is thick and makes it hard to trek through.

"Oh no, you don't!" Nick grabs me easily and falls into a nearby snowbank. Snow seeps through my coat, making it that much colder. "Think you can get away with that?"

"No!" I try to pull away from him, but Nick's grip is tight. His bare hand is like ice as it slips under my coat. "Too cold! Too cold!"

"You should have thought about that before throwing snow down my coat."

Nick rolls me on top of him out of the snow.

"I might be rethinking all of my plans with you this weekend," I say as a shiver racks my body.

"Not even if I promise to warm you up?"

"Maybe a hot shower?" I drag my nose along his cold one. "Something to warm us both up?"

"Bex, I plan on doing whatever you want this weekend."

"How did I get so lucky?" I whisper against his lips.

"You mean to find the most awkward guy on the planet and turn him into something not awkward?"

I shake my head. "You just needed the right person to appreciate everything you are."

"And do you appreciate me, Bex?"

"More than you will ever know."

More than I can put into words, because the feelings I'm feeling for this man are getting big. Big and scary and too hard to ignore anymore.

I just need to get my head and my heart on the same page. Because Nick is worth it.

He's worth everything to me.

Chapter Twenty-One

NICK

"Are you sure it's safe that we're out here?" I ask Bex on the short walk down to the pond behind the cabin.

Pine trees are covered in snow. Drifts cover the bases of them a few feet high. A light snow falls from the sky.

"Oh yeah. It freezes over early and won't thaw until May."

"Wow."

Bex has no right looking as sexy as she does as she walks up to the small, old shed that sits next to the pond. In a pair of black snow pants, a light pink coat, and a gray hat, she is ready for our game.

"I can't believe you have your very own pond out here for hockey."

Bex moves the goal from the shed into place in nothing but her snow boots. She really was made to be around hockey. "During the winters, my dad would love coming up here with a few of the guys for tournaments."

"Really?"

Poking my head into the wooden shed, I spot a few

pairs of skates and grab ones that look like they'll fit. It's always weird wearing another guy's skates, but I'll make do. Especially if it means Bex and I are out here together.

Lacing them up, I push off and do a few laps around the pond. Not the best-fitting pair of skates I've ever worn, but they'll do.

"They were epic. They made these ridiculous trophies that they would play for."

"What, like a frozen pond on one?" I ask, skating around her.

"No. They made them out of old glass tequila bottles. Soldered a metal bowl on top as the cup."

I bark out a laugh, breathing in the cold mountain air. It feels so nice to be out here and not worrying about playing in the All-Star game.

No hockey. No practice.

Nothing.

Just me and Bex.

"You know, this isn't you doing a good job of not thinking about hockey," I point out.

"No, this is okay. I don't have to make a single decision. It's perfect." Bex sits on the bench that looks like it was built for these tournaments, and laces up her own pair.

"Okay then. Why don't we play for something? I know we don't have our own trophy, but I'm sure we can come up with something."

Bex does her own lap before skating over to me. "I'll make you a bet."

"You've got a trophy over there?" I nod to the shed. "Because if so, yes. I want to win one of these tequila trophies."

"And if there's no trophy?" Bex skates around me. I shouldn't be surprised at how good her form is, but she's a great skater. She shrugs a shoulder as she comes to a stop in front of me. "What would you want to play for then?"

Skating over to the bank of the pond, I grab the two sticks and hold one out for her to take. I dig the small black disk out of the snow pile and shoot it toward her.

"What do you have in mind?" I hold the stick over my shoulders, resting my hands on it.

"Winner gets to pick what we do tonight."

"That's it?" I snort a laugh.

"Oh no, Nick." Bex walks her fingers up my chest. "In the bedroom."

I have to ignore the way my cock stirs in my sweat-pants. "Now you're playing dirty."

"Don't take it if you don't think you can win."

"Just because I'm a goalie doesn't mean I don't have skill."

"Then put your money where your mouth is, Nick," Bex whispers in my ear.

"You're on."

"How long are we going to play for?" I ask her.

"One period." Her voice is firm. "One period to deter-mine which of us is the better of the hockey players."

I skate over to her, tugging one of the long, braided pigtails that hang out from under her hat. Pink coats her cheeks from the cold air. I give her a quick kiss. "May the best person win."

"Don't worry, I will."

Bex skates off, grabbing the puck and circling me. It's hard not to stand here and just watch her. Why is it that everything this woman does wraps me up into her world, completely clouding any rational thought from breaking through?

"Getting cocky already?" I shake off the Bex-induced fog and match her skate for skate. It's different not being in all the garb I usually wear for the game. But when Bex shoots her first shot, I deflect it easily.

"Just saving it for later." She winks, not even fazed that she missed her shot.

Taking the puck, I head toward the center of the pond and make a show of my puck-handling skills. Not something that I get to do very often.

"Show-off," Bex laughs. "Shoot the puck, Nick."

"You can't rush a master," I tell her, easing her back slowly toward the lone goal at the edge of the pond.

I deke her out and put the biscuit in the basket.

"Would it be rude to celebrate?"

Bex rolls her eyes at me before fishing the puck out of the back of the net. "By all means, go right ahead. Because that's the only one you'll be celebrating."

"We'll see about that."

The game continues, Bex putting two in before I get another. Bex wasn't kidding about saving it for later. Her stick-handling skills are superb. I shouldn't be surprised because she's good with her hands. But watching the way she fakes me out and then shoots the puck into the back of the goal has me muttering under my breath.

"If I didn't know your skills, Nick, I'd be questioning your starting position with the team." Bex circles around the goal, celebrating her goal to put her in the lead.

"Ouch!" My breath comes out in a puff around me as I shoot the puck toward the center of our rink. "I can't help it if I am distracted by the cute winger."

Bex smiles at me, skating backward toward the center of the ice. "I'm not distracted by the sexy man in the goal. You need to get your head in the game. Or are you trying to lose?"

I skate toward her, making a move and grabbing the puck from her. "Do you really think I'd lose to you on purpose? Because from where I stand, this bet benefits both of us."

A sly grin tugs at the corner of her mouth. "Yeah, but it will be infinitely more fun for one of us than the other."

"That would be me."

I shoot the puck at the goal but Bex gets the tip of her stick on it and sends it wide.

"Damn. I'd say if managing the team doesn't work out, you have a future as a player," I tell her.

"Have you seen the badass women that play for the women's league? That Lydia Bishop is incredible. There's no way I could ever match her level of skill."

"Yeah, Troy is pretty proud of her."

"I'd say I'm surprised how much talent is in that family, but it's not all that much of a surprise."

Bex once again shows off her skills and trips me up to get another one on me.

"Damn it!" I shout in jest.

"Seriously, Nick. Is this the best you have?" Bex teases.

"In my defense, I usually am in the net the whole game."

"Maybe I need to talk to Coach Barney. Make you guys change it up at practice and skate in another position. Get an appreciation for what others do."

Bex has me distracted enough that she steals the puck. It's hard to focus as she skates. She's good, a certain gracefulness to the way she moves.

It distracts me enough to watch the puck sail past me into the goal.

"Yes!" She pumps both arms in victory as the timer in my pocket goes off in a loud shrill. "In your face!"

Bex does a lap around the pond, celebrating as if there is an invisible crowd there watching her. It's the cutest fucking thing ever.

Dropping my stick, I skate over to where she is and pull her down into a snowbank. The brightness in her face is mesmerizing. I don't think I've ever seen her look so happy, and fuck, it does something to me knowing I had a hand in it.

"Are you ready to concede?" Bex asks.

I shake my head. "I don't think I have to concede if you won fair and square."

"That's right I did. Pond Hockey Champ!"

I kiss her cold cheek. "Do you need me to make you a trophy?"

Bex nods. "Yes. In addition to winning the bet, I would like a trophy that says I beat the best goalie in the NHL in pond hockey."

"It's only because you're so sexy," I tell her. "It's hard to concentrate."

"If that's what you want to tell yourself, Nick." Bex kisses my nose. "I somehow managed to concentrate playing against you."

"I guess that makes you a better competitor than I am."

"Or maybe more determined to win." Bex waggles her head. "Now, about that bet…"

Chapter Twenty-Two

All afternoon, I have been driving Nick crazy. Little touches here and there. A light kiss with no heat behind it. I haven't missed the growls from him every time I brush by him.

It's only going to make it better.

Now that dinner is done, I'm ready to make good on my bet. One that will benefit both of us.

Nick, wiping his hands on the dish towel, is eyeing me as I saunter down the stairs. After a quick shower after the game, he changed into a soft, dark plaid flannel and sweats. Stubble lines his jaw. He looks so at home that it makes me want to stay here. To shut out the world and live here.

Dropping the towel, Nick takes slow steps toward me. Every dirty thought is swirling in my brain as the heat between the two of us ticks up another ten levels.

The lights are dim with a crackling fire providing warmth in the cabin. The wind shakes the panels of the windows as snow continues to fall outside.

"Sit on the couch."

Nick walks backward but keeps an eye on me. "I—" he starts.

"What I say goes tonight." I give Nick a gentle shove as he falls back with a soft oomph onto the couch. "The only answer is yes or no. Do you understand?"

A smirk pulls at his mouth. I wonder if he's going to say something else when he nods. "Yes."

"Good boy." I pat his chest, still covered with the material of his flannel.

Untying the belt on my deep-purple, silk robe, I let it fall to the floor in a pool of heavenly material. Nick's gaze takes in the lingerie I'm wearing—a black, lace bra that does nothing to hide how hard my nipples are and a matching thong that arches high over my hips.

His pupils are wide with lust. His cock is tenting his sweats. Watching him take me in has me wanting to slip my hand into my underwear.

But I don't.

Not yet.

"Like what you see?"

"You know I do." There's a bite to Nick's tone. He's turned on and I'm driving him crazy.

"Take a closer look."

Pushing Nick's knees apart, I stand between them. His eyes rake over my skin. I'm ready to combust under his heady gaze when I notice his eyes lock on to the small streak I rubbed over my stomach. It's so faint, you can barely see it.

That was the whole point—to make sure it didn't rub off before we got here.

"What is it?" Desire coats his voice.

Dropping forward, I rest my hands on his knees so he can take a closer inspection of my breasts. The scrap of material lent itself perfectly to my little plan tonight.

"Why don't you try it and find out?"

Nick licks his lips, looking up at me before resting his eyes on my cleavage. There's a small X of chocolate there. It was the only thing I could find to make this game work.

Nick's breath ghosts over me as his tongue licks a path up my chest. Tension ratchets up in my body, making my skin buzz and feel too tight.

It's the faintest of touches but has me dizzy with lust.

"Mmm. Fucking delicious." He darts his tongue back out for another taste.

Moving my hands to his shoulders, I push him back and he groans, licking his lips. I want to taste what he does. Instead, I stand and slowly undo the buttons of his shirt.

Each inch of skin exposed has me wanting to do this to him. To mark him up everywhere I want to taste him. But since I want all of him, it wouldn't be the easiest feat.

"I think you've been a good boy."

"I have?" Nick is practically drooling now. Biting down on his lip, he's noticing the marks I decorated all over my body.

"There's a lot more of these for you to find." I do a quick spin, showing him my back. "Every spot you find…"

"Yes?"

"I want you to lick the chocolate off. Taste. Bite. Nip. Suck. Whatever you want. I want you to leave your own mark on me."

Nick punches his hips off the couch, the hard outline of his cock obvious in sweats. Oh yeah, he likes this idea.

"Can I use my hands in the discovery process?" His voice has dropped an octave.

Leaning forward, I tug his earlobe between my teeth and give it a hard pull.

Nick is a force to be reckoned with during sex. He always makes me feel so good, that every time is better than the last. As much as this is for him, it's also going to blow my own mind when he finds that final X.

"Yes. But no ripping of any lingerie. This is handmade in London. I don't want it getting torn."

The look on Nick's face is sinful as he sits forward. The way his shirt hangs off his shoulders makes him look even sexier. Like he couldn't be bothered to finish undressing he was so out of his mind with need for me.

Nick takes his time, showering me with attention as he sucks on the spot just above my hipbone. Sinking my fingers into his hair, I let him set the pace. The nibbles and sucks are making me so turned on that I'm ready to throw my plans to the wind and ride him into oblivion.

"So fucking good, Bex. Mmm," Nick murmurs against the inside of my thigh now. A firm hand grasps my hip and pulls me down onto the coffee table. Leaning back on my elbows, I watch as Nick stands to his full height.

Taking my foot, Nick finds each mark and has his way with me. By the time he gets to my lace-clad pussy, he's blowing a breath of hot air over it, making me squirm.

"All these marks, Bex." Nick shifts direction and sucks a bruising kiss into the soft skin at my breast.

"Gah!"

"Mine," he growls. He nips again. "Fucking mine."

The possessiveness in his voice is overwhelming. "Yours, Nick. Mark me."

Firm hands push my legs apart as he breathes me in. "Is there a mark waiting here for me?" He brushes his nose over my clit, not moving the fabric of my thong.

"Why don't you take them off and find out?" I tease.

Grabbing the edge with his teeth, Nick pulls the flimsy material off and tosses it behind him. Being bare like this for him is intoxicating.

"Do you know how sexy you look like this?" Nick stuffs his hand into his pants and pulls himself out. I lick my lips as he gives himself a solid stroke. "Laid out like this for me. My bite marks all over you. Fuck, I could come just like this."

"No," I bite out. "You are not coming unless you are inside me. Now, Mr. Brooks-Young, I believe you have another mark to find."

"Yes, ma'am."

Dropping to his knees, Nick pulls my ass to the edge of the table and licks a stripe up my pussy. His tongue swirls through the wetness before licking off the chocolate just above my clit.

"Do you know how delectable you are? Your pussy and this chocolate? Heaven."

Nick dives back down and buries himself between my legs. Every nip and suck has me plunging further into the abyss of pleasure.

"God, Nick. I want to come. I need you inside me. Now," I command.

Shoving a hand into his pants pocket, he pulls out a condom and makes quick work of rolling it over his hard length.

"I could get used to this," I breathe out. "You at my every command."

Nick shucks the rest of his clothes before settling his weight over me. His cock lines up perfectly with my pussy as he gives a few pumps of his hips. "You mean me worshipping you, Bex? Worshipping at your feet like you deserve? I'll never want to stop this. Never."

Slotting the head of his dick against my opening, Nick pushes inside, slow and steady. Inch by inch, he fills and stretches me. I dig my nails into his back and my heels into his ass to draw him in closer.

I want to feel him everywhere. Not only the bite marks on my skin, but to etch him even deeper inside of me. A place I already know he will be for a very long time.

"Bex." Nick drops his forehead to mine, looking down at where he's entered me. "You look so good with me inside you."

"Fuck me, Nick. Hard."

Capturing my lips in a steamy kiss, Nick sets an unrelenting pace. The wood of the coffee table digs into my back. The bite of pain has me squeezing down on his cock with every punch of his hips filling me up.

Nick tears his lips from mine, shifting my hips up to deepen the angle. Seeing him tower over me as he holds me up throws me over the cliff.

Wave after wave of pleasure courses through me as I shout my release. His growls and moans have him picking up the pace. The heat surrounding us draws out every ounce of my orgasm. Sweat clings to my skin as my body floats through the best release I've ever felt.

"Bexley!" Nick shouts, tossing his head back as he fills the condom. His fingers are bruising on my hips as he continues pumping inside me through his own orgasm.

The pulsing beat in his neck is a rapid tattoo matching my own. Dropping my legs, Nick scoops me into his arms and settles us onto the couch.

We're still connected, and this tender moment after what we just did has me burrowing deeper into his hold. I've never felt as safe as I do in Nick's arms. This man has marked his claim on me, and I never want to relinquish it to another soul.

Nick peppers me with kisses as he cups my chin and pulls my focus to him.

"I think I'd like to play you in hockey again."

"Oh yeah?"

"I want to claim you forever." Nick traces an X over my heart.

I guess X really does mark the spot.

Chapter Twenty-Three

NICK

The fire crackles. The candles lit on the table waft through the cabin, permeating it with a pine scent. With my head in Bex's lap, this night is pretty damn perfect.

The way her fingers drift through my hair is lulling me to sleep. Snow has started to come down outside. It's a bubble I don't want to leave.

Everything about this weekend has been more than I ever expected it to be. I had no idea that when I started this thing with Bex that we would end up here. I've never felt more settled in my entire life. Being in the position I'm in, it always feels like I'm waiting for the next bad headline to hit. I don't know if it's because that's how it was growing up, but whenever Dad's team lost, people made sure I knew about it.

Bex makes it easy to drown out the outside noise. A bad game isn't the end of the world. I know that I'm a good player and have what it takes to help take my team to the next level. I guess all it took was for Bex to help me understand that.

"It's been a long time since I've been up here." Bex looks around, as if taking the cabin in for the first time. "Sometimes being here is too hard."

Grabbing her hand, I press a kiss to the center of her palm. "Is it because of your mom?"

She nods, looking down at me. A wistful look lingers on her face. "She loved it here. It was the place the two of us always came together. If Dad was traveling with the team, she'd bring me here for the weekend. We'd paint, go hiking, cook dinner together. It's all the little things that add up that can sometimes cause me to suffocate."

Sitting up, I pull Bex into my arms and kiss the top of her head. "Does it help to talk about her?"

"Sometimes."

Rubbing a hand up and down her arm, I want to try and bring this woman comfort. I have no idea what it's like to lose a parent, but I don't know what I would do if anything happened to one of my dads. Even the thought is too much to bear.

"Tell me about her."

"She's where I get my love of gardening. Even if I'm not the best, she always said growing things ourselves was the best feeling. When I grew my first tomato with her, I think I cried when I ate it."

I smile at her, imagining Bex doing just that. Under her tough exterior is the warmest, kindest woman I've ever met. As evidenced by her crying over something she grew.

"I don't know how she got me to grow anything after that, but I loved being with her. Since Dad was always with the team, I was her shadow. Cooking with her was my favorite because she said we could always try whatever we wanted. We made some pretty crazy things."

"Like what?" I whisper, keeping Bex close in my arms.

Bex's laugh comes out watery. "I remember one time

we made a marinara sauce that had grapefruit in it, because in my seven-year-old head, why can't two fruits make a sauce?"

"Was it as terrible as it sounds?"

Bex sits up, shifting onto my lap. Tears linger in her eyes. "Disgusting. But Mom ate it like it was the best thing in the world."

"She sounds like a great mom."

"The best," Bex tells me. "She would have loved you."

"Yeah?" I ask, brushing the tear that slides down off her cheek.

Bex nods. "She died before I turned thirteen and I hated it. I never got to talk to her about all the things I really wanted to. Boys. Crushes. Which college to go to. My first love."

My heart clangs around in my chest at the pain I feel for her. I wish I could take it away from her, but I know I can't. That it will never go away.

But if there's one thing I can do, I can be there for her during the hard parts. When it gets too overwhelming for her.

Because whether I like it or not or was even ready for it, I've fallen in love with Bexley Hart. This woman with the big heart that she doesn't show the world. Somehow, I'm the lucky bastard she's opened herself up to.

Brushing her hair off her face, I lean close, whispering in her ear. "Want to cook something? Maybe it'll be like she's here with us."

Clasping my cheeks in her hands, Bex gives me a tender, heart-wrenching kiss. I can taste her tears there.

"That sounds like the perfect idea."

I follow her into the kitchen to get out all the ingredients we need for dinner. Bex is quiet as she hands things to me and turns on the gas stove to start the chicken. It seems unfair that we have to head back to the real world tomorrow. All I want to do is stay here with her. Make this place our home and never leave.

I know we can't. But it doesn't mean I won't cherish every single second of our time.

The two of us work together like a well-known dance, like this is something we do together all the time. It's something that I spend more and more of my days thinking about. How Bex and I could have this permanently. Not just for a few short weeks, but longer.

Forever?

Is it too much to hope for that the two of us could have forever?

"Nick?" Bex breaks into my thoughts, pausing her cooking of the chicken.

"Yeah?"

I drop the knife, bits of garlic and onion messily chopped up on the cutting board. Bex is staring up at me, her tears gone. A smile of contentment is etched onto her face.

"Thank you. For this. I know it might seem silly, but this means a lot to me."

My hands are covered in garlic, but I don't care. Wrapping my arms around Bex, I tug her close and drop my forehead to hers.

"I will give you whatever you need, Bex. Always. Because..."

Should I tell her? Tell her I love her? That she's stolen my heart and I never want it back? Maybe it was always destined to be only hers, but there is no other person in this world that I'll ever feel this way about.

Fuck it. Life is short.

"I love you, Bex. I don't care if it's too soon or if you need more time, but I have to tell you."

"Oh, Nick."

The smile on Bex's face tells me everything I need to know before she kisses me. The kind that seals our love together in a way that will never be torn apart.

I'm thankful every damn day we ended up in that bar together. I don't know what I would do if I were to miss out on this with Bex.

Maybe we needed the guise of helping each other to get over our fears. Or maybe it's that we could only be ourselves with each other. That we felt safe enough to be our true selves.

"You are the most kind, gentle soul I have ever met, Nick. I don't think my mother would have found anyone more perfect for me than you, and that's why I know she would love you like I do."

I can't help the smile that spreads across my face. "You love me?"

"Of course I do. How could I not?"

I steal a quick kiss from her. "I love you, Bex."

"I love you too, Nick."

Ignoring the fact that dinner is cooking, I give her a slow, teasing kiss. One that tells her exactly how much I love her. That everything about her is what I want and need in life.

How did I ever get so lucky to find this woman?

Popping from the stove breaks our kiss, much to my dismay.

"I guess we'll have to continue this after dinner," Bex says, going over to stir the chicken. "I'd hate not to feed you."

"I could survive." I go back to my own chopping, but keep stealing peeks at Bex.

Tonight feels like one of those nights that I'll remember forever. I felt connected to Bex before tonight, but now? Now it feels different. Like each of us opened up a new part of ourselves to share with the other.

I have no idea what the future holds for the two of us. All I can hope is that when we share the news of our relationship, we can still have these quiet moments. I don't want to have to live our lives for public consumption.

I want this cabin. Spending the evenings making dinner together. Watching football during the offseason. Playing pond hockey together.

I only want Bex.

Taking the veggies over to her, I watch as she plops them in the pan and covers it with the lid. I bring her into my arms, burying my face in her neck.

"Thank you for giving me this part of yourself. For showing me this side of you, Bex."

"You're the only one I trust with it."

"I love you."

She shifts and peers up at me. "I love you too."

"Do you think you'll get tired of hearing it?"

Because I've only said it a handful of times to her, but I want to shout it from the rooftops. That I love this woman and she is mine.

"Never."

"Then I'll never stop saying it, Bex."

That is one promise I have no problem making.

Chapter Twenty-Four

NICK

BEX

Ready to get back on the ice?

NICK

I wish we were still back at the cabin

Me too

As good as it'll feel to get back into the swing of things, it was a nice break

Maybe we can do it again in the offseason....

Take more than a weekend?

Not play hockey on the lake. Do something else maybe...

Like...

Skinny-dipping

Fuck, Bex. I have practice

> Well then, you better practice hard and then come see me after

> For another reenactment of what we did in your office?

> Now who's the one making someone all hot and bothered?

> Guess you'll just have to wait for me until after practice

> Or I could take care of things on my own

> You better not. I want you ready for me

> Then get your ass to practice, Brooks-Young

> I'll do my best just for you

> <<kissy emoji>>

There's a pep in my step as I head into the practice rink. Even though All-Star weekend was a short break, it's enough to revive even the weariest of players.

And having spent the weekend with Bex, I couldn't be feeling any better. This far into the season, the bumps and bruises take longer to recover from.

Three days off was exactly what I needed.

Pushing open the door to the locker room, I head straight for my stall, oblivious to the fact that it's now deadly silent.

Looking around, all eyes are on me.

"Uhh, what's going on?"

Troy, Cash, and Noah all walk over to me. Their faces range from giddy to confused to stunned. What the hell?

"What the fuck, Nick? Were you ever going to tell us?" Noah asks, disbelief in his voice.

"Tell you what?"

"What do you mean, tell you what?" Troy mocks. "You haven't seen the news?"

"What news?" I ask, looking between the three of them.

Cash grabs his phone from the cubby above his locker and types away on it before thrusting it into my face.

Headline after headline of Bex and me are there. A photo of the two of us kissing outside of my condo graces each article.

Secret relationship between Black Diamonds GM and Goalie? What this photo could mean…

Bexley Hart seen kissing Colorado goalie Nick Brooks-Young

Love or lust? Let's break down the history of the relationship between Bexley Hart and Nick Brooks-Young

"OH FUCK," I whisper, scraping my hand over my face. I tap on one and wait for it to load.

Damn locker room being a dead zone.

When it finally pops up on the screen, I feel like I could be sick. There's speculation about our relationship, what it means for the team, how we got together.

I could keep reading, but I don't want to. What was a

private moment between the two of us is now splashed across the Internet for everyone to see.

"Do you have anything to say for yourself?" Cash asks.

"Is this why you're always running off and you're never at home anymore?" Noah asks.

"I...I..." I don't have anything to say for myself because I can't believe this got out. Practice starts in ten minutes, so there is no way I can go talk to Bex about this right now.

"Have you been laughing at us this whole time because we've been trying to set you up with someone?" Troy asks.

"Hey, I did want you to set me up with someone," I correct.

"Yeah, but you clearly didn't need it," Noah points out.

"So what, you just went for it with Bex instead?" Troy asks. "I have so many questions."

I wince. "Can we not talk about this right now?"

"Oh, we're going to talk about it," Troy tells me.

"Please don't tell Angie," I rush out. The last thing I need is my sister and dads finding out.

"Who do you think told me?" Troy drops a hand on my shoulder. "I'm surprised she hasn't texted you yet."

"Ugh." I bury my face in my hands. "Great."

The last thing I want is to look at my phone and see the family text chain. Knowing them, there's already a hundred unread messages.

"Alright men, listen up." Coach Barney's voice echoes through the locker room and all eyes turn to him. "You might have seen the news, but I don't want that to distract us. I want us to have a good practice before tonight's game."

I slink behind the guys that are now standing in front of me. I don't want to have to answer any questions right now. Not when I don't have any clue as to what is going on.

"Now that the All-Star weekend is behind us, it's full speed ahead. We're in a good position for the playoffs, and I don't want us to take our eyes off the prize."

Changing into my pads faster than usual, I find the guys lingering by the door as I head toward them.

"You know we're going to discuss this after practice, right?" Troy says.

"You heard what Coach said. Focus on practice," I tell them. "Can't you get them off my back, Cap?"

Troy laughs. "You think these guys will let up for anything? They won't listen to me."

"Fuck no," Cash agrees. "It's me or Piper. I know she wants to know the scoop too."

"Fine."

Walking down the tunnel toward the ice, I ignore everyone and head to the crease. Breathing in the icy air, this is one of the only things that will calm me down.

I've been doing this for so long that it lets me push everything else out of my mind and focus on the pucks coming toward me. On the drills I run with my coaches.

It feels good to be here. To get my legs back underneath me. Before I know it, the whistle is blowing and practice is over.

I grab my water bottle, taking a swig, and wait for the rest of the guys to head back into the locker room before following.

"Nick!" Piper's voice echoes down the hallway.

"Hey. What are you doing here?" I ask, dropping down to give her a quick hug.

"I was meeting with the old PT staff. Thought I'd drop by and see how you're doing."

"So everyone knows?"

She nods. "Sorry. That can't be easy."

Leaning back against the wall, I rest my hands on my stick. "All I want is to find out how Bex is doing."

"You haven't talked to her?" Piper screws up her face in confusion. "Why not?"

"I only found out before practice. I couldn't run up to her office without getting my ass handed to me by Coach Barney."

"It'll be okay," Piper reassures me, squeezing my shoulder.

"Will it? Because from what I've seen, it doesn't look like it will."

"Hey, don't go making any rash decisions. Talk to Bexley and see how she's feeling."

"I won't do anything rash. Listen, I gotta go."

"I'll see you after the game tonight, okay?" Piper gives me a smile before heading down the hall, not before stopping and turning back toward me. "And Nick?"

"Yeah?"

"You two make a really cute couple."

That pulls a smile out of me. At least one person is on our side. Not that the guys don't seem it, but I know it's going to put them in an awkward position with Bex.

The locker room is already clearing out as I head inside.

Thank God.

Stripping out of my gear faster than normal, I head straight for the showers. I let the hot water sluice down my body and relieve my tired muscles.

Of all the things that I thought would happen today, this wasn't one of them.

Not that I had any clue how we would announce our relationship to the world, but it wasn't going to be like this.

It's not something we planned on. I thought we'd have more time.

I take a deep breath as the water starts to run cold. It's bringing back all those feelings from childhood of being bullied. Of being the center of attention—the very last thing I wanted. The thought of playing tonight makes me feel sick. I don't want to face the ire of the fans if this isn't something they approve of.

Fuck.

Shutting off the water, I grab my towel and head back toward the locker room to change.

Troy, Cash, and Noah are still hanging around. For being a group of hockey players, these guys are some of the chattiest, most gossipy people on the planet. They have to know everything.

I step into a pair of sweats and hang my towel around my neck.

"Alright, let's have it."

Wrong thing to say apparently, because they all start talking over themselves before Troy quiets them with a quick slash of his arm.

"This won't get us anywhere, guys," Troy says. "What I want to know is why didn't you tell us?"

Fisting the ends of the towel, I try to figure out the best way to tell them. "It's not that I didn't want to, but I couldn't. I mean, fuck, she's the GM. It's not like I planned on this."

Cash eyes me. "Were you laughing at us the entire time we were trying to set you up?"

That has laughter erupting out of me. "Actually, that might be the reason we got together to start with."

"We were your matchmakers then?" Noah asks. "How?"

Thinking of that night brings a smile to my face. That

first horrible date and then the next, with my date cutting out before we even ordered. Texting Bex and meeting her in the bathroom.

"It turns out that we're both pretty bad at dating. We offered to help each other. But when the time actually came, it turns out we couldn't do it."

"Because you love each other," Troy states, matter-of-factly.

I nod. "I mean, yeah. I don't know how it happened, but it did."

Both Troy and Cash have a look wash over their faces that tells me they know exactly how it happened. Because they've been there before.

"You're right, Noah," Cash tells him. "We did set them up."

"In a roundabout way, yes."

"Should we start a business? Hockey Love for... losers?" Cash asks.

"Hey! I take offense to that."

Cash claps me on the shoulder. "Sorry, only thing I could think of. But we did good, right?"

"Yeah, you did," I confirm.

"What are you going to do now?" Troy asks. "I can't imagine this is going to be taken well."

Tossing my towel into my cubby, I grab my T-shirt and pull it on over my damp skin. It clings to me, but right now, I don't care.

"Honestly? I don't know. I've barely had time to process it or talk to Bex about it. We'll see."

The only thing I hope right now is that she doesn't break up with me because of it.

"You don't think anything will happen to her?" Noah asks. "Can they do anything to her?"

I shrug a shoulder. "I mean, she looked it up. There's

nothing in the by-laws of the league preventing this kind of thing."

"They probably never thought it'd be an issue considering she's the first female GM," Cash says.

"Do you think you'll get heat for it from other teams?" Troy asks.

"If they do," Noah steps in and says, "then we'll handle it as a team. No one is going to come after one of our guys for falling in love."

"Hey!" Cash wraps an arm around Noah's shoulder. "Now it's time to find somebody for you."

Noah pushes him off. "Nah. I'm good as it is."

Except I don't miss the note of longing in his voice. He wants love, but I'm not sure what's stopping him. Maybe because he's already met the right person? I don't know.

"Look,"—Troy drops down onto the bench next to me—"it's going to be a rough few weeks for you. But whatever happens, we're here for you."

Emotions clog my throat. It doesn't feel like the world is going to end. Sure, it's going to be hard, but I don't have to do it alone.

That's the difference between then and now. I have these guys. They're my family. I wouldn't want anyone else by my side while we weather this storm.

"Thanks, guys. I'm just sorry I brought this down on us."

"It'll be old news by the time we're in the playoffs," Noah says. "Just stay the course."

Stay the course.

It's hard to believe that this is where Bex and I are now. After overcoming all the weirdness and awkwardness together.

What we have is something that's real. That I love and wouldn't give up without a fight.

Shit is going to come at us from all directions. I know that and am not naive enough to believe otherwise.

But together, the two of us can get through it.

Because we're better together and can get through anything.

As long as we have each other.

Chapter Twenty-Five

BEXLEY

"No comment!" I shout into the phone, slamming the receiver down.

This day has gone from bad to worse. What I thought was going to be an easy day back after the All-Star break has turned into an epic shit show.

All because Nick and I made one stupid decision and someone caught us in the moment. Why did I think I could spend the night at his place and not get caught? One single kiss outside his building and everything has gone off the rails today.

Even with Anna holding my calls, the phone has been ringing nonstop.

"Sorry. I don't know how they keep getting in," Anna says, rushing into my office.

"They're vultures," I tell her. I rub the heels of my hands into my eyes, trying to make the headache go away. "God, I wish I could rewind time."

"Can I do anything to help?" Anna is standing in front of me, chewing on her lip. It's like she wants to ask the question everyone wants to know the answer to, but isn't doing so.

Thank God for that. Because I'm not ready for people inside the office to dictate my relationship with Nick.

I'm a masochist and did that all on my own. Nothing good ever comes from searching your name on the Internet.

Is Nick Brooks-Young sleeping his way to the starting goalie position?

Is Bexley Hart fit to lead the Black Diamonds?

Tell All: An ex of Bexley Hart's gives us the scoop!

THAT LAST ONE really cut deep. An ex from a few years ago detailed how I was a cold, ungrateful girlfriend who never made time for him.

If only I could give my side of the story.

That all he wanted was to use me for my name and success to sleep his way to the top.

I'm sure he got a pretty penny for his lies.

"Order in Thai for lunch and make sure I see Noah sooner rather than later. With Coach Barney. His meeting can't wait."

God, of all days.

With the trade deadline tomorrow, this is one meeting I wish I didn't have to have.

Noah Fields has always been our best player. But after Graham Fisher took him out earlier this season, he hasn't been the same. Even though he's only twenty-nine, a hit like that is hard to recover from.

I only wish I didn't have to ever have this conversation.

These are the parts of the job that I hate. Sure, I've traded other players before, but none that are as beloved as Noah.

He's been at the heart of this team since my dad drafted him years ago. But the writing is on the wall, and we have too good of a deal to pass up from Nashville.

With Paddock coming to us, it'll help build our defense to make a deep playoff run. I know he's been underutilized there, and with first round draft picks for the Knights to get Noah, I would've been crazy not to take it.

If only the offer was from another team.

It's only adding more fuel to the fire to make every fan hate me. On top of sleeping with the goalie, I'm cutting the most beloved player?

Yeah, it's a shit day and about to get even shittier.

"I can have them up here in five minutes." Anna is tapping away on her tablet. "Lunch is ordered and I'll bring it in right after your meeting."

"Thank you."

She spins on her heel and leaves my office, shutting the door with a quiet click.

Thank God for the blinds in here, because I could not stand the looks today. I got enough of them walking in, thinking I had toilet paper stuck to my shoe when I realized it was something else.

I take a few steadying breaths, trying to push all other worries aside to focus on what I need to do next. It's what Noah deserves. Not some half-assed *you're gone* because I'm too distracted by his best friend to give him the news in a more gentle manner.

A knock on my door can only be one person. At least Anna has prevented people from coming and going in here all day.

She should get a raise for that.

"Come in."

The minute the two of them walk in, the mood changes. Tension hangs thick in the air as I wave them over to my small sitting area.

"Hey guys."

"How you holding up, boss?" Coach Barney asks, dropping down into one of the seats.

"I'm fine." I wave him off. "I'm sorry to bring you both in here today, but we need to have a talk, Noah."

I address him, and based on the way he's sitting, he knows what's coming.

"I'm sorry to be the one to tell you this—"

"You're trading me?" he cuts me off.

I wince, nodding at him. "I'm sorry."

Noah pushes a hand through his brown hair, shaking his head in what I take to be disbelief. "I can't say I didn't see it coming. I wish I didn't, but I know I'm not recovering like I should be. Fucking knee."

I humor him with a laugh. "You're one of the best players we've ever had, and I wish things were different."

"All good things must come to an end, right?" A sad look washes over him and I hate it. I really do.

"I've got some numbers for you for people in Nashville that will help you get setup once you're there. The team wants you in San Jose, so they've arranged flights for you to meet with the team there."

"Wait, Nashville?" This time, it's a look of disgust on his face. "You're sending me to Nashville?"

"I've talked with Coach Rivers and he's a good man," Coach interjects. "You'll do well under him."

"But...Fisher is there."

"I wish it didn't have to be this way, Noah." Coach Barney looks sad as he holds his hand out to him. "You're truly a one-of-a-kind player and I know you'll only support your team once you get there."

Noah grumbles something else about Graham Fisher. There is no love lost between the two of them.

"Thanks, Coach."

"Thank you for all you've done for the Black Diamonds, Noah. We wouldn't have gotten the cup last year without you."

"Do you mind if we have a few words in private, Ms. Hart?" Noah asks.

Coach Barney stands, pulling Noah in for a hug before walking out of my office. His face is grim when he turns to face me, brown eyes heavy with sadness.

"I'm sure I'm the last person that should be telling you this, but treat him right."

"Excuse me?" His words have taken me aback.

Noah nods. "Nick is one of my best friends and one of the best people I know. He hasn't always had it easy, and I know being in the spotlight like this isn't going to be easy for him."

I soften at his words because I know exactly what he's talking about. My sweet, sweet man has never taken a shine to the public spotlight. Ever since he was a kid, he's hated it.

"I know. I love him, Noah. It might not look like it from the outside, but I do."

"It takes a special kind of woman to love him. And I know if he loves you back, you'll be the luckiest person in the world."

I stand, walking over to Noah and giving him a hug. "Thank you for taking such good care of him all these years. I promise, I'll look after him now."

Noah returns the hug. "Thanks. Now, wish me luck

because I'm going to need it since you're sending me to play with my archenemy."

I laugh, pulling back from him. There's a playful look on his face now. "I'm sorry. Just keep your head down and play hockey and you'll be okay."

"Thanks, Ms. Hart."

I wave him off. "Please, call me Bex."

"Thanks, Bex. I'm sure this won't be the last time we'll see each other."

Giving me a warm smile, Noah is out the door.

I collapse onto the couch. That went better than I thought, but it still wasn't easy. My phone chirps from my desk and I ignore it. Nothing good will come from picking that up.

Now back to the matter at hand.

Figuring out what to do about my relationship with Nick.

Chapter Twenty-Six

NICK

"Nick! What do you have to say about your relationship?"

"Did Bexley coerce you into a relationship?"

"How long have you two been sleeping together?"

"Nick! Do you really think you deserve your position at goal? Did you steal the job from Anderson?"

"Did your relationship with Ms. Hart contribute to Noah's downfall?"

Gritting my teeth, I ignore every single shouted comment as it comes my way. Normally, I smile and wave to the press that lines the entrance to the locker room. They're always here to catch us coming into the games. The pregame swagger, as they call it.

Except today, there is no swagger. Only anger. So much

of it, that I feel like I could explode on the first person that looks at me the wrong way.

Because of a late practice, and then Bex in meetings all afternoon, I haven't gotten the chance to see her. If they're shouting these kinds of comments at me, I can only imagine what she's suffering through.

This couldn't have happened at a worse time.

The noise of the locker room does little to help calm me down. Especially when I take in the empty locker now next to mine.

"Troy." I grab his arm as he passes by me. "What's with this?"

I point to Noah's empty locker.

"You didn't hear the news? He got traded."

"Fuck. Are you serious?"

Troy's nod is grim. "To Nashville. Bexley didn't tell you?"

"Why would she tell me that?" I follow Troy to our cubbies. Cash is already there, drinking his pregame smoothie that looks like grass.

"I don't know. Pillow talk maybe?"

I groan, wanting to beat my head against the locker.

"Seriously, Troy? Not cool," Cash calls him out.

"What? Not pillow talk, but I only assumed she would have told you."

"Nope. I haven't seen her since the news broke."

"Oh shit," Troy says, offering me a consolatory look. "That sucks, man."

"Noah really got cut?" I ask him. I look to Cash, who nods his confirmation. "Why didn't he say goodbye?"

Cash shrugs a shoulder. "You know how fast these things happen. Nashville has a game in San Jose tonight, so they wanted him there to start bonding with the team."

I wince. "God, he's going to hate playing with Graham."

That must have been what that reporter was talking about. What a fucking nightmare—them thinking my relationship with Bex had anything to do with it.

It feels weird, chatting with the guys and not having Noah here. Even though I haven't been playing long, Noah has been with me since the start of my tenure with the team. He helped ease the transition from college to the big leagues.

Going out onto the ice without him tonight is going to be a big change. I know things can happen in this league, and while I wish I could have talked to Bex about this, it's been a day.

One that I can't wait to be over.

By the time the game starts, I'm a ball of nervous energy. The vibe feels different to me. Maybe I'm picking up on something that's not there, but it's like everyone is judging me.

Judging every decision related to me and the team.

Judging my relationship with Bexley.

Hell, judging me as a person in general.

One of the guys from Vegas breaks off from the team and skates toward me.

The cocky smile on his face has me wanting to punch it off. "Think I could get her to spread her legs for me?"

"What the fuck?" I snarl at him.

"Will any player do? Or is she only hot for goalies?"

The sneer on this guy's face has me skating toward him, but Cash blocks my path.

"Don't. It's not worth it."

"Did you hear what he said?" I yell at him, trying to skate around him. I want to grab him by his ugly-as-sin orange-and-brown jersey and shake him. Bex doesn't deserve those words.

"No, but you need to get your shit together so we can win this game. You got me?" He gives me a hard stare, one that I'm none too excited about.

"Fine."

I watch as he skates backward toward his bench. What a dick.

I've got my eye on him. There is no way in hell I am going to let that fucker score tonight. Not after what he said about Bex. For the first time in my life, I wish I wasn't between the pipes. I wish I was out there with the rest of the guys so I could go after him. Getting kicked out isn't on my list of things to accomplish tonight, but man, do I want a piece of that guy.

My focus is shot during the game. All I can think about is not letting that douchebag score. I block a few of his shots, but let in two easy goals. I need to get my shit together fast, or this is going to turn into a runaway.

There's a whistle for a stoppage in play when it happens.

The douchebag—I have no clue what his actual name is—skates over to me, a smarmy grin on his face. "She's looking pretty sexy up there. I should show her what it's like to be with a real man. Not whatever excuse you're pretending to be."

Fuck that.

Dropping my gloves and stick, I charge after the guy and put all my weight behind taking him down.

"Say that again." My knuckles collide with his jaw with a splitting crack.

Ringing in my ears blocks out all other noise as the guy squirms under me to try and get a hit in. It glances off my pads before I'm being hauled off him.

His nose is dripping blood onto the ice as two of his teammates hold him back.

"Serves you right, you asshole!" I shout at him.

"Fuck you!" He spits onto the ice.

"You think you're some macho guy for talking about women that way? Fuck you!"

"Nick!"

Troy and Cash are in my face, pushing me away from the opposing players. From the looks of the bench, the coaches are holding back the players from starting an all-out brawl.

Fuck. I can't believe I did that.

Troy and Cash are both still in front of me, angry glares aimed my way.

"What the hell is wrong with you?" Cash asks. "You can't do that!"

A glance toward the bench tells me the backup is going in. The anger of the fog clears as I realize I'm being kicked out of the game.

Fuck.

Boos echo around me as I grab my gear and skate off the ice. Add my stellar play in tonight, and getting kicked out is the cherry on top of my day.

I've never been so on edge in my life. One minute, I'm stopping the puck, and the next I'm going after the guy from Vegas who said vile words about Bex.

The minute I hit the locker room, I'm stripping out of my gear and throwing it—with a little too much force— toward my locker and then hitting the showers. The steam helps to calm my racing thoughts. My knuckles are banged up from taking a swing at that guy. I hope he has it worse than me.

Should I have gone after him? No.

But when he said Bex will spread her legs for any

player, I snapped. The last thing I want is for anyone to think so little of Bex. Even if we weren't together, I wouldn't want them saying something like that.

I've seen how hard she works. About the hardest damn working person in the league, but I'm biased. She's in the office early, stays late, and comes to just about every away game there is unless she has meetings with the league.

Did I bring this down on her? Is this all because of me? I hate that that's the thought I keep coming back to.

It's been nothing but a shit storm since news broke about the two of us. The guys are still giving me grief about it, but half the team is looking at me like I'm going to be the one cutting them if they're not up to snuff.

And to top it all off, Noah is gone.

My best friend and roommate. Traded to the Knights because of his less-than-stellar play this season after his injury.

Having to go play with the guy that took you out? I can't imagine that's going to be easy for him.

"Where are you going?" the team assistant asks as I straighten my tie.

"To watch the rest of the game."

He shakes his head. "Oh no, you don't. The only place you're going is to the family suite because we don't want anyone seeing you. You're not to speak to any press tonight, do you understand?"

"Why?"

"Did you take a puck to the head, or did you forget you just got kicked out of the game? There is no way you are in the right headspace to talk to the media," he tells me.

Fuck.

This night has only made things worse. Instead of keeping my eyes on the prize and focusing on the game, I let the words of one player get under my skin.

If I can't keep my shit together, it's only going to keep this in the press longer.

"You need to calm down, and Coach will come get you when he is ready to talk to you."

Fan-fucking-tastic.

If I'm not benched through the end of the season, it'll be a miracle. Stalking out of the locker room, I head to the friends and family room.

The walls are a light beige with pictures from the team covering the wall. There is a small space for kids to play with various toys. It's something I've never really paid attention to, having that small area for kids.

Will I get that one day? Will I get it with Bex, or will everything good the two of us have go up in smoke because of the outside pressure?

The game plays on the TVs attached to one wall as I collapse onto one of the couches, closing my eyes and pinching the bridge of my nose to stave off the impending headache.

At least the sound is off so I don't have to hear anything they're saying about me. I check the score from time to time, and while Reeves, our backup, is holding his own, we're not putting any points on the board.

If we hadn't already clinched our playoff spot, I'd feel even worse about getting kicked out. Not that it's an excuse, but I let my team down in the worst possible way.

Who knew being in love could be this hard?

"There you are."

I pop my head up at the familiar voice. "Ang. What are you doing down here?"

She kicks my legs off the couch and drops down next to me. "Family, duh. I have a pass to be here."

I roll my eyes and lay my head back on the couch. "Just what I wanted—my big sister to come and give me shit."

"Nah, no shit from me." Angie wraps her arm around my shoulders and pulls me into her side, keeping me there. "I can only imagine what that guy said to make you go after him."

"I can't even repeat it, it was so bad."

"You know you can't let them get under your skin. Bex wouldn't want it."

"I know."

"Good. Now, once you're back from however long you're benched—"

"Hey, we don't know that yet," I cut her off.

Angie laughs, patting my arm. "If you don't think Coach Barney is going to bench you for at least ten games, you're out of your mind."

Sometimes I hate having a sister so close to the game. Instead of being comforting, she only confirms my worst fears.

"I hate it. I let the team down; I let Bexley down. Everything I'm doing seems to be screwing up the lives of the people I care about."

"Well, that's just wrong," Angie tells me. "No one thinks that."

"None of this would have happened if I hadn't started dating Bex."

"Would you be any happier if you weren't dating her right now?" Angie throws back at me. "Because even though you never told us, which I will give you so much shit for when you're feeling better, I don't think I've ever seen you so happy."

A smile tugs at the corner of my mouth. I don't want it to, but it's there. Thinking about Bex has my heart starting and stopping in my chest.

After everything we've been through together, there's no way that I wouldn't want to be with her.

Bexley is the only person in the world that seems to get me. To know what it was like to grow up in the shadow of a famous parent. She's warm and caring, and so damn sexy, it hurts to look at her sometimes.

"How do I make this better?" I ask my sister.

"You apologize. Whether it's to the team, Bex, whoever it needs to be, apologize. But don't back down for falling in love with her. I learned that the hard way."

I was too young when my sister got together with Troy to understand what was going on when our dads found out about them. But I know Angie wouldn't be the person she is today if it weren't for Troy.

"Do you think I should go to the press?" I ask.

"Do you want to?" Angie asks, pulling back with wide eyes. She knows why I hate being in the limelight. How hard it was growing up for me. We're so different, that it sometimes surprises me we come from the same person.

"If it'll help Bex, yes."

Angie nods. "Okay. Then do it. But take a few days and think over what you want to say, because if you don't come off as honest and direct, it'll make things ten times worse."

"Being in love sucks."

Angie drops a kiss on the top of my head before standing. "It does sometimes. But if what you have with Bexley is the real thing, then it's worth it. You'll get through this, Nick. I know you will."

With that, she's gone.

I turn my gaze back to the game and lose myself in it. The third period is better, but we can't dig ourselves out of the hole we got ourselves in and lose 6-4.

Fucking great.

Chapter Twenty-Seven

Everything is a disaster right now as I listen to the boos rain down in the arena. I don't remember the last time a game turned this ugly.

The Black Diamonds are a good team. We never stoop so low to get under the skin of the other team. We're not gunning for any one player. We play good, clean hockey.

Tonight?

Tonight it's like another team entirely is out there. I've lost track of the number of power plays we've given Vegas. Chippy moves here and there.

And now Nick got thrown out of the game?

What the fuck?

All I want to do is scream.

The look on his face when he went after that guy? I've never seen Nick like that before. It's like he was an entirely different person altogether.

What in the world happened down there? One minute, he's in the crease blocking a goal and the next he's skating after a player and going after him.

I repeat…what the fuck?

"The press are going to have a field day with him," Cassie comments next to me from her seat in the executive box.

"You think I don't know that?" I snap. "What in the world has gotten into them tonight? This is a disaster."

"I can think of one thing…" Cassie shifts in her seat and pins me with a knowing glare. "Can you really not think of what would set him off?"

"Oh God."

I bury my face in my hands, letting my hair fall down around me so I don't have to see anyone.

Did Nick do this because of me?

When the news got out, the world started pressing in from all sides. The press is having a field day, going through and finding any photo of Nick and me throughout his playing career and analyzing it for hidden meaning.

A few GMs have reached out stating I should break off my relationship to prevent any further damage to my reputation or the team's good standing. One or two suggested I resign to stop any further disgrace I may bring upon myself.

The league, while they can't do anything because there's nothing stating I can't date my player, said I need to lie low while they go into damage control mode.

Worst of all, I haven't heard from my dad. I know he saw the news because his assistant said he would not be issuing a statement at the time. *No comment* might be the worst thing he could possibly say.

I haven't missed the looks I've been getting. The sneering and the catcalls have all been too much. It's turning into a dumpster fire and I haven't the faintest clue on what I should do.

"Something's gotta give, Bex. The team can't keep continuing like this."

The horn sounds to end the second period. "God, we still have more hockey left to play?"

It's one of the few times I wish we could end a game early, even if we're losing. The less chance we have out there on the ice to screw ourselves over, the better.

The bright side? We're leading our division and guaranteed a playoff spot.

"What am I supposed to do?" Tears well in my eyes as I watch the fans leave their seats during intermission. Dejection hangs heavy over my head. Over the fans' heads. We've never been in a situation like this. This isn't the kind of hockey the Black Diamonds are known for. "I've messed everything up."

"C'mon."

Cassie sidesteps me and grabs my hand, pulling me behind her. The other executives in the suite are casting morose looks my way. I can't blame them when the team is down 5-2 and we lost our starting goalie.

"Out. Let's go, out!" Cassie barks, kicking a few women out of the restroom as she kicks the door shut behind her and flicks the lock.

"What in the world are you doing?"

Cassie leans against the wall, giving me an assessing look. "You haven't messed everything up, and you need to get that out of your head right now."

"Then why does it feel like that?" I cross my arms. I feel like it's the only thing I've been doing—trying to ward off all the unnecessary attention.

"Because you're in the thick of things right now. Until you wade through the muddy waters you've stirred up, it's going to be a shitty time."

"Would a statement help?" I ask Cassie.

"It would only bring more speculation down on you.

They'd take what you say and twist your words around until you're the most hated person in the league."

"I already am," I sigh. "Maybe I should just end things with Nick. It's what everyone is calling for. That and my job."

Cassie moves in front of me and grabs my shoulders. "Is that what you want?"

"No."

It's one of the easiest questions I've answered.

Maybe that's why this has been so hard. Not one single person has come out in support of my relationship with Nick. I know what the pundits are saying on the sports news shows. They're saying I somehow coerced Nick into a relationship because of the age difference. Or how he used me to secure his starting spot with the team.

I don't know why it's so hard to believe that two people happened to fall in love, regardless of their positions with the team.

"All I want is to be with Nick," I mutter, glancing down at my shoes. "I didn't mean to fall in love with him, but I did."

The thought of breaking his heart is too much for me to bear. I didn't plan on falling for him, but he's the only person who understands me. Knows what it's like to grow up in my shoes.

I've never been with someone so kind, so tender, and someone as loving as him.

"I know, sweetie. Until then, you need to put on your big girl pants and not let everyone get you down. Take a few deep breaths, cry, scream it out, but when you go back out there, you're Wonder Woman. Nothing fazes you."

"Do I get the bulletproof cuffs?"

"Only to ward off the ugly words of the press." Cassie

smiles at me. "And just in case, I'll send Cash to do a **PR** event with Puck and the public will eat it up."

I snort laugh, as she wraps an arm around me and steers me back toward our box before the start of the third period. "Who knew Cash Williams would become our saving grace?"

Cassie gives me a knowing look. "Me. It's why you pay me the big bucks."

NICK

FAMILY MEMBERS COME and go as the guys slowly filter out of the locker room after the game. I don't miss the way no one looks at me.

I need to find a way to fix this and fast. Even if I'm suspended, I have to apologize to the guys. I've never lost my cool like that during a game.

The family suite is quiet now, only me here. Stuffing my hands in my pockets, I start to pace, working through what I'm going to say to Coach Barney.

He's the type of person you never want to disappoint. And that's exactly what I did today.

"Nick."

It's not the voice of Coach Barney like I was expecting.

It's Bexley.

The set of her shoulders. The deep frown sitting on her face. The wetness ringing her red eyes.

She's a mess. All because of me. Fuck.

"C'mere."

I open my arms and she falls into them, holding on tight.

"What were you thinking?" Bex whispers against my chest.

"I couldn't let that guy get away with talking about you like that."

Bex pulls out of my arms and leads me over to the couch, pulling both of us down.

"Nick, I don't need you fighting my battles for me."

"But—"

"No buts." She puts a single finger over my mouth to cut off any further conversation. "I've probably heard a lot worse than what he said, and it certainly won't be the last time."

"Bex, I love you. They shouldn't get away with that."

Bex gives me a watery smile. "Then next time don't get kicked out of the game and win it to prove that you're better than they are. Don't stoop to their level."

"I don't think I'll be playing in the next game."

She rolls her eyes at me before burrowing into my side. I feel the breath she lets out and pull her even closer.

We both need this. Need each other to be close to get through these next few weeks.

"You won't be."

"Do you know that for a fact?"

Bex nods against my chest. "I ran into Coach Barney. I delayed your meeting with him until tomorrow, but it's a done deal."

"Fuck."

Bex turns to face me and wipes the tears from her eyes. "I have to support him in this decision, especially when it comes to you."

"I know, Bex." I wipe the last few stray tears from her face. "I hate what this is doing to you."

"Me? Look what it's doing to you, Nick. You're not like this. Sometimes I think..."

"Think what?" Dread settles in my gut. I don't like where she's going with this.

"That maybe we'd be better off if we weren't together."

My heart cracks open in my chest. If it came spilling out onto the floor right now, it wouldn't surprise me.

"No. Hell no. That is not the answer, Bex."

"I…I don't want to. But what if it is easier? No one would be coming after you or the team, and they'd leave me alone. Leave all of us alone."

"What, so give them what they want?"

"God, I don't know!" she yells, standing and pacing in front of me. "Why is this so fucking hard? Couldn't you be, I don't know, a teacher?"

I smile. "I mean, you know that's what I want to do when I'm done with hockey. Maybe I could be done now."

That gets a bitter look from her. "If you think for one minute I'm letting you quit, you're wrong. I will fight you to the ends of the earth to make sure you stay with this team."

"Okay." I throw up my hands and grab her hand to pull her back into my arms. The place she belongs. "As long as you don't quit us, then I won't quit hockey."

"What are we going to do, Nick?"

"I don't know, Bex. But we'll figure it out together."

Chapter Twenty-Eight

BEXLEY

I hate this. From the moment I stepped inside our offices, there's been nothing but whispers and stolen glances at me.

It's like all the work I did before doesn't matter now. They can only see me as someone who is dating one of the players. God, it makes me feel cheap. Like nothing I've done has made a single difference to the team.

I should just quit now and get this over with. Let them have someone who they don't have to question every day, but I don't want to let them win.

Even now, after coming back to my office from meeting with Cassie—more damage control—the looks haven't stopped. Nick's suspension only added more fuel to the fire.

Cassie has been working overtime to try and squash all the rumors flying around. I've been trying to ignore them, because after one more comment about me sleeping with any of the players, I was going to explode.

"Anything that needs my attention, Anna?"

Anna shoots up from her desk with a consolatory look

on her face. "Nothing important, Bex. There is someone waiting for you in your office."

"Did I miss a meeting?" I groan. The last thing I need is another meeting. Especially one that I might have forgotten about in the chaos of everything going on.

"No. This one was a last-minute addition to your day. I know you said nothing unexpected, but he's a hard man to say no to."

Of course whoever is behind my office door is hard to say no to.

"Thanks. Hold my calls."

"Already done." She drops back down to her desk and goes back to clacking away on her keyboard. Shouldering open the door, the person sitting at my desk is the last person in the world I expected to see.

"Dad. What are you doing here?" Shock doesn't even begin to describe what I'm feeling when I see him. "Aren't you supposed to be in Spain?"

"I think you needed me more than Spain did." He stands, striding around my desk to pull me in for a bear hug. "It'll still be there in a few weeks."

I sigh, wrapping one arm around him. I can't remember the last time he's come to my rescue. It's not that I needed it—I'm thirty-six after all. But it's nice to have a familiar face when I'm in the thick of things here.

"I know you heard the news."

"I did."

Dad walks over to the couch and takes a seat, kicking his feet up on the table. For being gone for a few months, he looks good—skin maybe a little too tan, salt-and-pepper hair, and a bit of a belly now. I'm sure he's been eating and drinking his way through Europe. But his eyes tell me that he's happy. Even if he had to make a detour from his trip, the look on his face tells me he's happy he's here.

"And? No opinions on it?"

"Why do you need my opinion, Bex? You're an adult and can do what you want."

I drop down into the chair across from him, dejection sitting heavy in my gaze. This is why he flew all this way? Not exactly a comforting conversation. "But…your statement to the press. You had no comment."

Dad laughs and pats the couch next to him, beckoning me to him. I don't move from my spot. "I had no comment for them. It's a personal matter. Why do they need to get involved?"

I roll my eyes at him. "It's not just a personal matter. It involves the team. And you. It's about as personal as it gets."

"How does it involve me, Bex?" He eyes me.

"Because you own the damn team!" I shout, exploding up from my seat and pacing in front of him. "Everyone is saying I've tarnished your legacy and I'm a disgrace to the game and are calling for my head on a platter. Do you know what that's like? Because it fucking sucks, Dad. And you have no comment? Really?"

Dad pins me with a stare that would have a lesser person cowering in front of him. Having been on this end of my fair share of these, I'm not scared. I'm not that same teenager sneaking out that he caught breaking curfew.

"That stare won't work on me."

"Fine." Dad laughs. "I should've known better. But why on earth would you think that you're a disgrace to me?"

"They said disgrace to the game," I mutter, picking at an invisible thread on my blouse. "Not you."

"Bex. You have done no such thing to my legacy."

"I haven't?" I look up at him. "Then why are you here?"

It's been two weeks since the news broke. Two long weeks of enduring nothing but snide comments and tasteless rumors the press have made up. I thought if we could weather the news cycle, all of this would blow over.

But it hasn't. It's like the longer I stay quiet and don't release a statement, the worse it's gotten.

No comment will only get you so far.

And the fact that it's affecting Nick and getting him suspended? I don't want that to happen again. It can't happen again because now it's affecting the team.

"Because I messed up."

"How?" I shuffle over to the couch and drop down beside him, tucking my legs up under me.

"Bex, when I heard the news, I realized I dropped this team on you and then left."

I suck in a deep breath, because…yeah. That's exactly what he did. My dad has owned the Black Diamonds for longer than I can remember.

"I know you've been with the team in some capacity since you graduated from college, and I knew you were ready to handle it, but that doesn't mean I made it easy on you."

"It's been hard," I tell him the truth. "Some days I wonder why you chose me at all."

"Oh, Bexley." Dad wraps an arm around my shoulders and pulls me in close. "There is no one that I have more faith in than you. This team means as much to you as it does to me. That's why I knew you could do the job."

"Really?"

I don't look at him, because tears are already starting to gather in my eyes.

"Really. I didn't do a good enough job of being there for you growing up. Of telling you how proud of you I was. After your mother died, it was easier to get lost in hockey. Hell, I had no idea how to handle a teenage girl dealing with her own grief while trying to manage my own."

"I don't think I would have let you help me. I was pretty hard to handle back then."

Dad laughs, pressing a kiss to the crown of my head. "You were always so resilient back then, but now, you don't need to be."

"It's the only way I know how to do this job."

"And this is where I failed you. You can show the world who you really are, Bex."

"Yeah?" I sneak a peek up at him. "And who is that?"

"You are strong-willed, have a heart of gold, and are one of the kindest, most genuine people I know. I'd hate to see you lose your heart because your head gets too caught up in how you have to be to do this job."

That's exactly what I've done. I've been training to do this job since I first stepped foot in this building. When I finally got the job, I saw the looks, heard the whispered comments that I only got it because of my last name.

I did everything I could to make myself look like I deserved this job. Getting too wrapped up in my head, especially now, I've lost sight of the big picture. Of what I really want.

I want this job. I love it. But I also want Nick. I'm letting everyone else under the sun determine my future. It shouldn't be that way.

"I'm glad you came back, Dad. I really missed you."

"I'm sorry I didn't come back sooner."

Leaning back, I look up at him. "When are you going back?"

"I'm going to stay for a little while. Jerry has his jersey number retirement ceremony coming up."

I nod. "Why don't you do it? I'm sure he would love that."

Jerry was one of the greatest Colorado players of all time, and Dad played with him for a few seasons before he called it quits. He has more of an attachment to him, so it doesn't bother me in the least to pass the torch to him.

"But I want you out there on the ice with me."

"Okay, Dad."

"Good. Now, why don't you tell me about Nick?" He stands, walking over to the cabinet where I keep the liquor. The same one he had in his office before he gave it up.

"Dad! It's not even noon. You can't be drinking now."

He shrugs a shoulder. "Eh, I'm on Spain time."

"And it's not five in Spain either."

"I'm old, Bex. Let me have my vices," Dad chides. "Now, I want to know about this man you're dating."

I roll my eyes at him, garnering a laugh.

"You know you remind me of your mother when you do that."

"You mean get annoyed with you?"

"She always used to get after me for pestering you to tell us things. It was like squeezing water out of a rock she would say."

"I miss her."

"I do too, Bex. But she would be so proud of the woman you've become."

It's those words that give me the confidence to move forward. I realize just how much I've withdrawn into myself these last few weeks. This isn't what she would've wanted for me.

I might have fallen in love with the wrong guy, but it doesn't make what we have wrong. And instead of everyone making me second-guess myself, I need to dig deep and find her courage. To face the press and all the fire that is raining down on us.

Because on the other side of it is my heart.

Nick Brooks-Young.

Chapter Twenty-Nine

NICK

"Feel good to be back on the ice tonight?"

I chance a glance at Troy, who is putting on his pads for the game tonight.

"It does and doesn't."

It's been a long two weeks serving out my suspension. With the team being on the road, it made it even harder to watch us struggle. We made it through, winning half the games. Can't say it's going to make the highlight reel of my career, but that fucker deserved it.

I'll always stand up for Bex.

At least I had her by my side. We tucked ourselves away in her house, trying to limit media exposure. I hate that we have to hide what we have now that everyone knows. But the judgment is still raining down on us.

"Still weird that Noah's gone?" Cash asks, breaking through my thoughts.

I nod. "Yeah. He's the reason I'm even playing hockey. I thought we'd play together our entire careers."

Troy claps me on the shoulder. "It's always an adjustment. But Paddock will be good for us."

"I know. He's a monster out there on the ice."

Paddock is the reason that we did as well as we did while I was out. He really was being underutilized in Nashville.

"All thanks to me." Cash gives us a cocky grin.

"Your head doesn't need to get any bigger," Troy points out.

"My head isn't big. We're just great out there on the ice. He knows exactly where he's supposed to be. It's a thing of beauty watching him play."

"Yeah, yeah. Sometimes it's really hard to like you." I laugh.

"Nah, you love me." He ruffles my hair before grabbing his gloves and stick.

"Gentlemen, listen up." Coach Barney's voice cuts through the pregame chatter and everyone quiets down. "We have the ceremony before the game. Jerry is one of the best to ever suit up for the Black Diamonds, so let's get out there and show him the respect he deserves."

"Yes, Coach," everyone chimes back at him.

Grabbing my jersey from my locker, I pull it down over my pads and grab my helmet, stick, and gloves.

I amble down the tunnel and when I step onto the ice, every worry I've had flees my head. Right now, it's only hockey. Going through my pregame ritual, I get myself in the game. I know there will be a lot of pomp and circumstance with Jerry here, but I don't need to worry about that.

When the lights go down, I follow the rest of the guys to stand in a line behind the red carpet that's been rolled out for tonight.

The man of the hour and his family walk out with Bex and her dad behind them. My eyes follow her every move, but hers stay focused ahead. I'm sure she doesn't want to draw any unnecessary attention to us.

Standing here on the ice gives me the chance to assess Bex's dad, the team owner.

Stephen Hart. He's a force to be reckoned with. I met him briefly after I was drafted, but the man scared me shitless. I was fresh out of college and worried about getting drafted and earning my place with the team.

Now? Now, he scares me for an entirely different reason. Because I want to be someone that is worthy of his daughter. I know Bex loves him, so his approval means everything if I'm going to be her boyfriend.

Boyfriend.

Somehow that word doesn't seem to fit what Bexley and I have together. Doesn't fit everything that has been going on between us these last few weeks.

It's been hard. Really fucking hard. Trying to get people to accept our relationship hasn't been easy. Hell, I still haven't introduced her to my family. *Officially.*

I've blocked out most of his speech before a video montage starts playing of Jerry's career here. Getting antsy, I'm shifting on the ice, trying to stay loose for the game. Stephen and Jerry are talking and laughing as the video rolls on.

It's easy to see the camaraderie the two of them have. I don't know how long they played together, but looking between Cash and Troy, it's something we have. Something this whole team has.

It's one of the reasons I love this team. Every guy is always there for one another. Even when times are tough, as they feel like now, we're there for each other.

By the time it's over, complete with guest appearances from past players, the crowd is on their feet. Hopefully this energy will carry us through the game.

"I'm proud to announce that no other Black Diamond will ever wear the number eighty-seven again," Stephen booms out as fabric drops from the rafters with his name and number.

The two men share a hug before Jerry takes the mic.

"It's good to be back, Black Diamonds fans. It's been a long time."

If possible, it gets even louder in the arena. We really do have the best fans in the entire league.

"I was blessed to get to play my entire career with Colorado, and let me tell you, there is no better organization than this one. They lead with their heart, always putting every single person on the team first."

His words strike me like a lightning bolt.

Lead with their heart.

It's exactly what I haven't been doing. I've been so wrapped up in my head about what everyone else thinks, that I've pushed what I want to the side.

Why am I letting pundits and sportscasters determine my future with Bex? We've been playing it scared instead of standing up and fighting for our relationship.

Bexley is standing behind the two of them, looking gorgeous as ever. But even from my spot across the ice, I can see how tired she looks.

I hate how much this has been affecting her. That the press is calling into question her dedication to the team.

Fuck it.

I make a decision. I don't give a shit about anything else right now except for her. Going against everything I know, I go for it.

I lead with my heart.

I close the distance to where Bex is standing, and her eyes go wide as she sees me.

"What are you doing?" she hisses.

"What I should have done to start with."

Taking Bex in my arms, I tip her to the side and plant a kiss smack-dab on her lips. I can feel her hesitance in my arms. But then she wraps her arms around my neck and kisses me back.

It's the best kiss of my entire life because for once, I'm not worrying about another person. I'm putting Bex first. Giving the middle finger to every naysayer that is sure this won't work for whatever reason.

I don't give a shit about any of it right now as I pull back and stare down at a stunned Bex. Stunned, but smiling.

Setting her back on her feet, the crowd comes back into view. The team.

Shared expressions of disbelief sit on all of their faces. It's so quiet, you could hear a pin drop.

Okay, so maybe I didn't exactly think this one through.

"Uhh, Nick. Got something you'd like to share with the fans here?" Jerry asks, a knowing smirk on his face.

"I didn't mean to steal your thunder," I tell him.

"Oh no. I want to know what's going on now. Please, share." Jerry walks over and holds out the mic, his smile getting bigger with each step. Dropping my gloves, I take it from him.

Crap. Now all those nerves are coming back in full force. I guess it's now or never.

"Sorry for stealing your thunder, Jerry," I acknowledge, before shifting my attention to the crowd. Bex links her fingers with mine and gives me an encouraging squeeze.

I can do this. I can do it for *her*.

"Jerry's words tonight got me thinking. About leading with your heart. Some of you might have seen the news about the two of us together."

That earns me a collective laugh. See, you can do this, Nick. Deep breaths.

"Bex and I love each other. It seems like every headline tries to discredit the love the two of us have. Using one another to get ahead. It's fake. Too much of an age gap. None of it means anything to us. We know what we have is real. And instead of showing you that our love is real, we've been hiding because we've been scared."

Another squeeze from Bex.

"We love each other. That's it. End of discussion. Continue your speculation all you like, be my guest. It's not going to change the love we have for each other."

"Yeah! You tell 'em!" Cash cheers out from his spot on the line and starts clapping.

It spreads like a wildfire. The cheers and whoops from the crowd grow louder with each second and, fuck me, does this ever feel good.

"Oh my God," Bex whispers. Looking down at her, I watch tears well in her eyes as her hand covers her mouth. "Nick. I can't believe you did that."

"Like Jerry said, lead with your heart."

Bex's smile is so bright, it could power the whole of the arena's electricity for the night. "God, I love you."

"I love you too."

"Excuse me, Bex?" The ref skates over to us, an annoyed expression on his face. "Listen, the game is supposed to start in a few minutes. Can we move this along?"

"Sorry about that, Marshall. We'll clear the ice."

Giving Bex one last kiss, I hand the mic back to Jerry and get a bear hug from him before they leave the ice. Bex waves to everyone as they continue cheering for her, and I skate toward the bench.

"About damn time, Nicky." Troy elbows me in the side. "About damn time."

I don't care what any other person says. If anyone doubts our love now, well, they don't get a say in it.

Because it's me and Bex. The love I've always wanted.

What more does any person need?

Chapter Thirty

NICK

I laugh at how similar my dads have become. They're basically the same person now.

POPS

Jinx!

ANGIE

Ignore them, Nick. I want to meet Bex.

DAD

See if we invite you to dinner, Angie.

ANGIE

I'm the firstborn, therefore your favorite

See if I bring her now

DAD

Back to my original question…why haven't you brought this girl home before now?

POPS

I think the correct term is woman

DAD

Fine. Woman

ANGIE

Are you two texting us from the same room again?

DAD

No! I'm in my office

POPS

…and I'm in the kitchen now

ANGIE

<<crying laughing gif>>

DAD

Don't make fun of your dads

ANGIE

You two make it so easy

Can we get back to me?

DAD

Yes, sorry.

POPS

Tell us more about her

> You can meet her tonight

ANGIE

You're no fun :P

> You all better be on your best behavior and not scare her off

POPS

Us?

DAD

We're offended

ANGIE

They have officially morphed into one person. Should we call you Dops or Pad?

POPS

Is it too late to disown them?

DAD

I don't think we can when they aren't living with us

POPS

Too bad.

> And now I'm considering disowning all of you

DAD

Best behavior. Promise, Nick

POPS

Cross my heart, hope to die, stick a
needle...wait, do they really stick a needle
in your eye?

DAD

You've been teaching too long

I'll see you at 7

TROY

I have one appointment after practice and I
miss all the good stuff! 36 unread
messages might be a new record for
the fam

ANGIE

I'll fill you in later <3

I DON'T THINK I've ever been so nervous in my life. When I asked Bex if she wanted me to pick her up, she said she had to drop her dad off at the airport before coming over.

I think she wanted to squeeze in a little more time with him. He's been nothing but supportive of the two of us. After that big game, a lot of opinions have changed. Even though I don't care about any of them. The only ones that matter are ours, and those of our families and close friends, and they've been nothing but supportive.

Except as I wait for her now, I'm scared shitless to have her meet my family. Officially. I know she's met Angie in passing at games, but that's it.

"When is Bex going to get here? Can I call her Bex?" Troy asks, dropping down onto the sectional next to me.

"You can call her Bex." I laugh.

Of course he's already met her. But does he know Bex as my girlfriend? No. I should probably be more worried about any discomfort he might have, but I don't. Because I love her.

This is the first chance we've all had to get together since the news broke of us dating. I wanted her to meet them sooner, but with our schedules, it's hard.

"Can I tell you it might be weird having her around at first?" Troy asks, looking sheepish.

"It's okay. I felt weird being with her at first too."

Not that it took long to get over it. Bex is the one person in the world I can truly be myself with. It's like the two of us were just drifting along, waiting for one another.

It doesn't matter how far apart we are in age. It doesn't matter if no one but us understands what we have. This thing between us is real. The kind of love I see every day in the people around me.

I'm thankful that I was lucky enough to find it with Bexley.

"Can I say I'm glad you found someone?" Troy tells me. "Because sometimes I would think you're lonely and needed someone to love you and that big heart of yours."

"I promise, I'm not. I love Bex, and she's the perfect woman for me."

She's the chaos to my calm.

The outgoing to my shy.

The strength to my every weakness.

"Yup, you're in love." Troy slaps my knee before getting up.

It's then the doorbell rings.

"She's here!"

Angie's voice echoes through the house as she runs to the door. Leaping over the couch, I try to get there before her and manage an arm around the waist to pull her back.

"Get off me!" Angie shouts. "I want to get the door."

Troy is laughing behind us as Dad walks right by us to

get the door, muttering something about us still being in high school.

"Hi, Bexley," Dad says, ushering her inside. Bex looks casual today in a Black Diamonds long-sleeved shirt and yoga pants. I told her the dress code was laid-back for Sunday dinner, and I love that she didn't feel the need to dress up to impress us.

I think my family is impressed enough as it is that I'm dating someone, let alone Bex.

"Hi, Mr. Brooks-Young."

"Please, call me Alex."

Bexley eyes me before shaking his hand. "Alex. It's nice to meet you."

"Carter. Bexley is here!" Dad shouts.

"I'm right here." Pops comes around the corner, brushing a hand down his sweater. A new sweater that he was not wearing earlier. I love how much of an effort he is putting into this. "Hi Bexley. I apologize for this brood of mine. I think I'm the only one that has some manners."

"Hey!" we all snap at him. Troy and Angie bicker over each other and Dad makes a comment about how he welcomed Bex inside.

Grabbing her hand, I pull her toward me. "Please tell me you're not rethinking this whole thing."

Bex eyes my family as they head into the living room, a smile sitting on her face. "They're wonderful, Nick. I've always wanted a big family."

As chaotic as my family is, I love everything about them. And I can't wait to have Bex be a part of this.

"Well, get ready. Because they are going to welcome you with open arms."

I give Bex a quick kiss before taking her hand and leading her into the living room. Everyone has their spot on a couch, and Pops is bringing out glasses of wine.

"Bexley, we're very happy to have you here," Pops says, offering her a glass of wine.

"Can't say I'm not shocked still," Troy tells us, grabbing his own glass. "The guys want me to tell them how tonight goes."

"Of course they do." I drop down onto the couch and pull Bex down next to me. She turns into my side and I wrap my arm around her.

"I wasn't going to tell them. Well, Noah maybe since he won't get to be here to get the details."

I feel Bex wince next to me and I squeeze her shoulder. "He'll be just as annoying as you, even in Nashville."

"Ouch!" Troy feigns hurt.

"Can I ask how you two ended up together?" Pops asks. Dad is sitting next to him, his hand resting on his leg and Pops's arm wrapped around his shoulders. Even now, after being together for so long, they are still outwardly affectionate in their love for each other.

This is why I wanted to find someone so badly. To have what they have.

"Please feel free to leave out any details we don't need to hear," Dad says with a wince. "I don't need to be scarred for life."

"Dad!" Heat flames up my cheeks. "Don't make this any harder than it needs to be."

Bexley rests her hand on my thigh and it settles me. At least someone in the room has some common sense right now.

"Nick and I happened to be at the same bar one night when he had a disaster of a date—"

"Did everyone witness how bad Caroline was?" Troy asks.

"Let them tell their story." Angie swats at him. "I want to hear it."

Troy gives her a chagrined look before pressing a kiss to her cheek.

Bex continues. "He looked so disheartened afterward, that I went to talk to him and things grew from there. Lunches together. Date nights. A weekend away. I know it's not the easiest relationship because of who we are, but I wouldn't have gone into this if I didn't believe there was something real and lasting here."

Something inside me settles. Bexley's words turn off every dial that has been running on overdrive for the last week. Things are going to be hard. We're going to have to defend our relationship at every turn.

But for this woman? I will go to the ends of the earth to defend it. Defend her. Because no matter what the outside world says, our love is real.

Pops and Dad share a look. One that I've seen many times. One that is full of love and mutual respect for the other. It's the kind of love I grew up witnessing. That I knew I wanted. I wouldn't settle for anything less than that.

"It takes a special kind of person to accept all the madness of my life, and Bex knows it."

"It really does," Pops and Angie agree. Having lived through it already, they know.

"And the league is okay with this?" Dad asks, ever the pragmatist.

I nod. "There's nothing that states we can't be together, so if anything, it's frowned upon. But we don't care."

"If you need us to make a statement after your big proclamation, I can get all the guys on board," Troy tells me.

Hearing Troy's unflagging support is more than I ever needed to have. If we have the captain on our side, I think we'll be okay.

"Calm down, Troy," Angie tells him. "One thing at a time."

"Can I talk to Nick alone?" Troy asks.

"We'll get dinner on the table. C'mon." Dad waves everyone into the kitchen.

Bex gives me a quick peck on the cheek. "I love you."

"I love you too."

Troy shifts on the couch, moving closer to me. I sink farther back into the cushions, letting them support my weight. It feels easier to breathe now that everyone knows about us.

No more hiding. No more lying.

It's a freeing feeling.

Troy leans over and pulls me in for a hug, taking me by surprise. "You're like the brother I never had. I love you, Nick, and you have my full support."

Tears well in my eyes as I grip on tight to the back of his shirt.

"Thanks, Troy. I needed to hear that."

Growing up, it felt like all I had were my dads and Angie. When the times got hard, when the outside voices got too loud for me, I didn't have anyone else I could turn to.

When I first met Troy, I was a surly high schooler who only wanted to study. But when he joined the family, I didn't realize how good it would feel to have another person to go to. I didn't always want to burden my dads and sister. Troy stepped up and has been there for me in every way since.

He's the best brother I could have ever asked for. He slaps me on the shoulder as he pulls back, wiping at his own eyes.

"Whatever you need, I'm here for you."

"Thanks, Troy."

"And look, your family already loves her."

I look to the dining room to see what he sees. Bexley laughing with my dads as they set the table together. It's like she's always been here. I don't know why I ever worried about how easily she slotted herself into my life.

Bexley is the perfect person for me. She accepts me for me and all my quirks. Having weathered the storm, I know that the two of us can face anything that comes our way. That's all I can ask for.

Bex and I together. It's all I've ever wanted.

And now? I have it.

Epilogue

"Your Colorado Black Diamonds are Stanley Cup Champions!"

The crowds erupt into madness. I'm hugging everyone that I can reach in the box. We did it. We fucking did it.

Back-to-back Stanley Cup Champions.

The ice is a blur through my tears as I watch the team celebrate. As I watch Nick celebrate. It's a strange feeling, winning it this year compared to last.

Last year was incredible, winning it for the first time as the GM of the team. Now though?

It feels different winning when it's not only your team but also the person you love down there. The pride I have for this team and Nick is unmatched.

After everything that happened, the team rallied. They were able to push all the noise out of their locker room and focus on the only thing that mattered.

Hockey.

"Congratulations, Bex!" Alex pulls me in for a hug. "Well done."

"Thanks. That means a lot coming from you," I tell him.

"Is it going to be a competition of who has more trophies now?" Angie comes up beside her dad. "Because I don't think I can handle that with you three."

"Nick and Troy might, but I *never* would." He laughs.

Carter pushes him ahead of us as I smile after them.

I laugh as I follow our team rep who has come to get us to go down onto the ice after the celebration. One perk of being the GM? I get to go out on the ice for the presentation of the cup.

As soon as the suite is empty, I take a breath. Tears flood my eyes as I take in the weight of this moment. It feels different than last year. Almost like I appreciate this win more because it was hard fought. I had to make some hard decisions this year with the team, and while the fans might not have seen it at the time, it got us here.

This team is my life. My found family. The place where I spend the majority of my time.

To see the success of that with the win being celebrated by Colorado fans everywhere? I don't know if I'll ever get over that.

Heading down toward the elevator, the only person waiting for me is my dad. He's bursting with pride in his navy blue Black Diamonds pullover and vest.

"Well done, Bex. I am so proud of you. Your mother would be too."

I squeeze him tight to me. "Thank you for believing in me."

"You didn't need it. You got here all on your own."

"Mr. Hart. Ms. Hart. Congratulations." The elevator attendant welcomes us inside the car and we head down toward the ice. Even inside the elevator, I can hear the fans cheering.

"Thank you, Cole. It feels good."

His smile is wide. "Makes me proud to work for you. You run a good ship here."

"Thank you."

My emotions are all over the place as the doors open and we head down the tunnel toward the ice.

"Go on out there," Dad tells me.

"You're not coming?"

"It's your moment."

I rush over to give him one more hug before heading onto the ice. "I love you."

"I love you too. Now go do the Hart name proud."

Walking onto the ice, I stay close to the boards. The guys are celebrating as the cup is brought onto the ice. It's a thing of beauty. Even more so because I know our team's name will be etched into it again.

Every player's name on it for the rest of time. Their contribution for helping to get us to this moment.

It's hard to hear the announcer as he congratulates the losing team and then moves on to talking about the Black Diamonds.

It's not long before he is calling Troy forward to accept the cup on behalf of the team. The moment he picks up the cup, fireworks brought onto the ice explode behind him. "We are the Champions" starts playing as he lifts the cup over his head to start his lap around the ice.

"Bexley, do you have a few minutes?" Paul, one of the network broadcasters who is on the ice conducting postgame interviews, taps me on the arm. It's hard to tear my gaze away from the guys. Especially as I finally lock eyes with Nick.

Work, then Nick.

"Sure thing."

"Congratulations on a fantastic playoff run. The Black

Diamonds looked incredible out there. How does it feel to win back-to-back Stanley Cups?"

I smile up at him. At the crowds that are cheering as the cup is passed around from player to player.

"I never thought this was something I would see. We have a talented team, but we're not alone in that. It's a fight to get every win in this league, and we never take those for granted. To be at the top of the hockey world again is an incredible feeling."

"You'll have a target on your back to get back here next year."

"We'll focus on next year later. Right now I want to celebrate this win with the team. They deserve it."

"How do you feel about the word dynasty being thrown out there?" Paul asks.

"That's something for another day. I'm here to support my team and give them the best chance to win the cup. And we did that."

The reporter holds a hand over his ear to try and hear himself talk over the chaos in the arena. Not a single person has left.

"A lot of people called into question your ability to lead this team when they discovered you were dating Nick Brooks-Young. What do you have to say to them?"

"I'll get back to you once I'm done celebrating the Stanley Cup win for the second straight year. Thanks, Paul."

His jaw drops as I stride away. That felt good.

Not good.

Fucking great.

That should hopefully shut up every naysayer out there. The comments about what Nick and I have are still there. But they aren't as loud as they were earlier in the season.

And now? Now they don't bother me.

What Nick and I have is real. We know what we mean to one another, everyone else be damned.

Speaking of…

Nick skates over to me, cup hoisted over his head, with the most beautiful, heart-stopping smile on his face.

"Got room to spare a kiss for me?"

His entire face is glistening under the championship hat he's wearing.

Holding onto his pads, I press up onto my toes to meet him for a kiss. The sweetest, best kiss of my life. Because despite all the odds, the two of us are here, having weathered the storm.

We could've caved and done what everyone else wanted us to do, but we didn't. There is no one else in this world that I would walk through hell and back for than this man in front of me.

As Nick goes to hand the cup off to another one of the guys, he skates back over to me, lifting me into his arms. "I don't think anything will ever top this," he tells me.

"What about another win next year?"

Nick looks around, a shocked look on his face. "Bex, don't jinx us. We only just won."

"Hey. I'm thinking big picture. Back-to-back? And that block to save the game from going to game six? Nick, that was incredible."

The smile lights up his face. Taking off his hat, he drops it onto my head, spinning it backward. "I knew you'd like that."

"Maybe I should give you a bonus for it."

"Oh yeah?" Nick quirks a brow at me. "What kind of bonus? Are you allowed to do that?"

Leaning down, I press a kiss to his cheek, mindful of

the eyes on us. "I'm thinking more of the kind that only you get."

"Oh yeah?" I feel his fingertips dig into my sides. "Like what?"

"Like licking champagne off of me."

"Fuck, Bex. You cannot tell me that while we're still on the ice."

I wiggle out of his arms and walk back toward where the rest of the team is now greeting friends and family. "Well then, better get these celebrations going."

NICK

"IT'S MY TURN!" Paddock shoves Cash out of the way and takes his turn drinking champagne out of the cup.

"Nicky! You're up next!" Paddock shouts, wiping his lips.

Warmth buzzes through my veins. The Black Diamonds rented out the entire bar for our celebrations. It's nearing one in the morning and not a single person has left.

Spotting Bex across the bar, I grin as she wiggles her brows at me as I step up to the cup and take a hearty sip of lukewarm champagne. "Shit. That's terrible."

"Probably the best damn thing you'll ever drink though, right?" Troy asks, curling an arm around my shoulder.

"Fuck yeah!" I cheer, causing all the guys around me to explode in whoops and hollers.

It's been like this all night. No one wants to leave.

We'll only get to be together like this once. With the

offseason now upon us, guys will move on and change teams. I want to savor this moment.

Music crackles through the speakers. Drinks are flowing. Lights are flashing overhead from the dance floor. Guys are crammed into booths with loved ones.

"Having fun?" Bex slinks over to me, wrapping her arms around my back, resting her chin there.

"More, now that you're here."

"I think you're doing just fine without me."

"Hey Bex!" Cash calls, interrupting the two of us. "Your turn!"

He points to the cup, the gold liquid floating in the top.

"There's no way I can drink from that!"

Troy shakes his head. "You have to. Otherwise you'll curse us for next year."

"Oh, fine." Except she's beaming as she heads over to the large cup and takes a sip. Pulling out my phone, I snap a quick picture because fuck, is there anything better than seeing Bex like this?

She's free. And open. Everyone loving on her exactly the way it should be.

"Hell yeah!" Troy fist-bumps her as the guys clap her on the shoulders.

As soon as she makes her way over to me, I clasp her cheeks and lean down to capture her lips with mine, savoring the cool feel of them and the taste of champagne against them.

"Mmm. So fucking good," I mutter against her. "How'd it taste?"

"Not as good as you."

Laughter burbles out of me as I tug Bex to a booth to join some other guys.

The night seems endless, like it'll go on for hours. Even after the lights turn on, no one leaves. That is, until my eyes get heavy and I can barely hold my head up anymore.

"C'mon. Time to get you home," Bex says.

I nod, a sleepy feeling taking over. Wrapping my arms around her, I let her lead me out to the car she hired for the night. Every guy has one. The last thing she wants is anyone making any stupid decisions tonight.

As soon as we're in the backseat of the car, I lay my head down in Bex's lap.

"Someone's tired," she purrs.

I nod, closing my eyes and burrowing in closer to her. "Long night."

My entire body aches in the best way. All I want is to be in bed with Bex. At this point, I need sleep more than anything else.

"I'm so proud of you," she tells me, scraping her fingers along my scalp. "You're incredible, Nick. The way you were moving on the ice tonight? You were a machine out there."

I look up at her. Nothing but love and pride is oozing out of her. "I didn't want to lose it for you."

"Even if you did, it would be okay," she whispers.

"Winning it is better though."

A small grin tugs at the corner of her beautiful smile. "It really is."

By the time the car pulls up in front of Bex's house, it's after four in the morning. Exhaustion hangs heavy between the two of us.

Too many drinks and celebrations have us heading to her room and collapsing into bed.

Bex kicks off her shoes and snuggles into her pillow. "You know, it finally feels like I don't have to prove anything to anyone."

"You know what I've always said about you."

"Oh yeah?" She yawns. "What's that?"

"You're the best of the best."

"I can say the same about you too, Nick."

"On top of the world together, Bex."

A place I hope we get to stay. Because this feeling right now? I want to bottle it up and never lose it. Getting to celebrate the team win AND have Bex?

I never thought it was possible.

"I love you, Bex. I'm so proud of you and everything you've done."

"I love you more, Nick."

Damn straight. Together, we'll always be the best of the best.

No matter what.

Want more of Nick and Bex? Read on to find out how they're spending their offseason…

BEX - ONE MONTH LATER

"I didn't think you'd actually agree to this," Nick tells me, grabbing the neck of his shirt and pulling it over his head.

"You should know by now, Nick. I mean what I say."

Pulling the thin straps of my dress down, I slip out of it. I feel, more than see, the slow perusal of Nick's eyes over my now naked body. It's one of the first free weekends we've had since winning the Stanley Cup that we were able to come out to my cabin.

And I intend on making good use out of every last second.

Diving into the water, the cool water is a balm to my warm skin. The pine trees sway in the wind, casting long shadows over the lake, protecting us from the sun.

Nick's teeth are digging into his bottom lip as I break through the water, wiping the drops from my eyes.

Sometimes, it's still hard to believe that the two of us made it here. After the chaos of our relationship being splashed across the sports world, it seemed like the media noise would never end.

But with a Stanley Cup win under our belts, it seems like the press is backing off.

Finally.

Nick looks relaxed as ever as he shucks what remaining clothes he's wearing and jumps in after me.

I don't have enough time to ogle his body, but I know it. Every freckle. Every ribbed muscle. I could draw his body from memory alone.

God, I love this man.

Watching him swim toward me, his eyes bobbing above the water? I can see every dirty thought playing through his mind.

The one I know is there?

Skinny-dipping with his sexy girlfriend.

Definitely one of the better ideas I've had.

"Took you long enough."

The second Nick makes it to me, I wrap my legs around his waist and hold on tight. Water droplets cling to his eyelashes. His blue eyes are filled with lust. Something that he can't hide with his growing erection between my legs.

"I think I can make it up to you."

Nick presses his lips to the corner of my mouth, eliciting a moan from deep inside me.

"Mmm. Please do." I dig my fingers into the soft, wet strands of his hair at the nape of his neck. "You really do need to make it up to me, Nick."

"Tell me what you want, Bex."

I love how much Nick loves pleasing me.

"You, Nick. Only you."

Nick slants his mouth over mine in a hungry kiss. After a long drive out this morning, Nick went for a run before we came out here. I've been needy for this man since the minute we stepped out of my house this morning.

The buzzing in my ears grows louder as Nick trails his lips down my jaw and tugs my earlobe into his mouth.

My nipples are hard as diamonds, brushing against his muscular chest. My nails are carving half moon patterns into his skin as I cling to him.

"I plan on doing nothing but making love to you all night." Nick thrusts his hips forward, his cock growing hard, even in the cool water. "I need you."

"You have me."

Not wasting another moment, Nick reaches between us and lines himself up before pushing inside.

"Gah!" I shout, not caring how loud I am.

Still in the shallow part of the lake, Nick grabs onto my ass and moves me over him. Ever since we started going without condoms, it's been even better.

Feeling his hard, bare length inside me drives me wild. Heat burns white hot inside me as I continue rocking over him.

Eyes that I love so much are staring up at me, urging me on. And when Nick slips his hand between the two of us to strum my clit, I damn near erupt.

"I'm almost there."

"That's it, Bex. Come for me."

Nick swivels his hips in the way he knows I love.

This is what I love about being with him. Even though we're familiar with each other, we still know how to drive each other wild.

And the way he thrusts inside me takes me over the edge.

"Yes!"

Throwing my head back, I hold on for dear life as my orgasm washes through me.

"Fuck." Nick's blunt fingers dig into me as he continues

pumping his hips inside me until I feel his release. "Fuck, Bex!"

Nick holds me to him as we both come down from our highs.

"I never want to leave this lake."

"You might turn into a prune," Nick whispers against my neck, gently pulling out of me.

"Don't care. I wish we could spend all our time out here."

I lean back, exposing my naked chest to the sky as Nick holds me in his arms. I've never felt safer than I do when I'm with this man.

"I think the team might miss us."

"I don't care," I whine. "I just want to be with you."

We don't get much time during the season. Coming out for an indulgent weekend in the mountains? It's almost unheard of.

"I'm not going anywhere, Bex."

Sitting back up, I hug Nick to me. Skin to skin. Not even the water could get through us. This is the way of love being with this man.

"I know. I love you, Nick."

"Not nearly as much as I love you, Bex."

Never in a million years did I think I would find my person on my team. On the Black Diamonds. Nick is more than a decade younger than me. There's no reason this relationship should work between the two of us. Yet, somehow, we fit together like two puzzle pieces.

"Are we going to argue over who loves who more?" I quirk a brow at him, sifting my fingers through his wet hair.

Without warning, Nick dunks me under the water. I come up a sputtering mess.

"Hey! That's not fair!"

"It's a game I'm willing to play. Because you will not win, Bexley Hart."

"Oh yeah?" I swim out of Nick's arms toward the center of the lake.

He nods, chasing after me. "You will not win this game of who loves who more. Because I will always win. No one can love another person more than I love you."

My heart stutters in my chest as Nick catches up to me and wraps himself around me again. Our legs kick together in the deeper waters.

The sun is brighter here without the shade of the trees to protect us.

"You can win for today, Nick Brooks-Young. But this is up for debate."

"A debate I'm willing to have."

"One we'll both win because we love each other."

I seal it with a kiss. Being with him is the easiest thing in the world. I don't care what anyone says about our relationship. The people who matter, support us. That's all that counts.

It's the two of us. We're the best of each other. The best of the best when we're together.

And that's all we'll ever need.

Author's Note

BOOK NINETEEN IS OUT IN THE WORLD!

Bex and Nick are here, and man, did these two give me a run for my money! I loved how their story unfolded and hope you loved it as much as I did. One of my favorite things about writing is writing strong, female characters. I want them to take up space in a place that they might not belong. And for that reason, Bex is one of my favorite characters. I mean, a female GM in a world of men? I only hope we see it one day.

Thank you so much to all of my amazing author friends for being along on this ride with me…especially Lily, Claire, Swati, Maria and so many others that are too many to name. The friendships I've made these last few years are one of my favorite parts of the business. And my very favorite person gets her own mention…Tina Snider. She's my favorite person in this world and I love her more than she loves Louis! Thank you to Trish and Menotah for beta reading and helping me make this book the best it can be.

To all you readers out there…thank you for cheering on the Black Diamonds and me! Your support means the world to me, and I love getting to meet you and hear from you! To my Street Team…thank you for always shouting about my books to the world. And to The Silver Society —

y'all are one of my favorite places to be on the internet, so thanking you for making it the best place on the internet.

<3 Emily

Also by Emily Silver

Colorado Black Diamonds Hockey

Best Kept Secret

Best Laid Plans

Best of the Best

Best of Both Worlds - coming October 31

Nashville Knights

Game Misconduct - Marcus and Harper's story, coming February 2025

Dixon Creek Ranch

Yours to Take

Yours to Hold

Yours to Be

Yours to Forget

Yours To Lose

Yours To Love - a newsletter freebie

The Denver Mountain Lions

Roughing The Kicker

Pass Interference

Sideline Infraction

Illegal Contact

The Big Game

Standalones

Off the Deep End — a MM sports romance

The Highland Escape - coming August 15

Merry in Moose Falls - coming November 21

Love Pucked - a sapphic hockey romance, coming early 2025

The Ainsworth Royals

Royal Reckoning

Reckless Royal

Royal Relations

Royal Roots

The Love Abroad Series

An Icy Infatuation

A French Fling

A Sydney Surprise

Get the trope guide on my website, or

scan the QR code to read my books now!

About the Author

After winning a Young Author's Award in second grade, Emily Silver was destined to be a writer. She loves writing inclusive stories, with strong heroines and the swoony men who fall for them.

A lover of all things romance, Emily started writing books set in her favorite places around the world. As an avid traveler, she's been to all seven continents and sailed around the globe.

When she's not writing, Emily can be found sipping cocktails on her porch, reading all the romance she can get her hands on and planning her next big adventure!

Find her on social media to stay up to date on all her adventures and upcoming releases!

www.ingramcontent.com/pod-product-compliance
Lightning Source LLC
Chambersburg PA
CBHW030124010826
48973CB00002B/408